A Scot To Have AND To Hold

Once Upon a Scot Series
Book Two

by Maeve Greyson

ARE YOU SIGNED UP FOR DRAGONBLADE'S BLOG?

You'll get the latest news and information on exclusive giveaways, exclusive excerpts, coming releases, sales, free books, cover reveals and more.

Check out our complete list of authors, too!

No spam, no junk. That's a promise!

Sign Up Here

www.dragonbladepublishing.com

Dearest Reader;

Thank you for your support of a small press. At Dragonblade Publishing, we strive to bring you the highest quality Historical Romance from some of the best authors in the business. Without your support, there is no 'us', so we sincerely hope you adore these stories and find some new favorite authors along the way.

Happy Reading!

CEO, Dragonblade Publishing

Additional Dragonblade books by Author Maeve Greyson

Once Upon a Scot Series
A Scot of Her Own
A Scot to Have and to Hold

Time to Love a Highlander Series
Loving Her Highland Thief
Taming Her Highland Legend
Winning Her Highland Warrior

Highland Heroes Series
The Guardian
The Warrior
The Judge
The Dreamer
The Bard
The Ghost

CHAPTER ONE

Dunstaffnage Castle
Western Scotland
September 1275

"WHOSE WOMAN DID ye dally with this time?"

"Shut it." Ross MacDougall shoved aside the smirking guard and pushed through the heavy oak doors of the main gathering room. An eerie lack of conversation among those loitering along the walls slowed his stride. Every man's focus locked on him, following his progress to the head of the hall. But it wasn't their stares setting him on edge. Nay, 'twas the smugness blighting their faces. Those sly grins rubbed his hairs the wrong way. These men knew something he did not. The ominous feel of an ax about to fall filled the air.

Ross tossed away the bothersome feeling with a roll of his shoulders. They could all go straight to hell. As a mighty *Gallòglaigh* warrior, brother to the constable, and unit commander in his own right, he owed these fools nothing.

"I see Lachren Martmullen took it easy on ye. The last man caught ogling his wife got his legs and arms mangled for his troubles." Alexander MacDougall, Lord of Argyll, invited him closer with an amused tilt of his head. "Tell me, Ross, did ye know who her husband was, or did ye just not give a shite?"

"Yer summons, m'lord?" Ross ignored the barb and grudgingly proffered the expected bow but refused to be baited—even by his liege. His head ached, his broken nose throbbed, and the split in his lip burned like a fiend. Nor would he discuss his lapse of judgment in front of all these grovelers who had nothing better to do than kiss the MacDougall's arse. "I believe yer missive mentioned a reward for a task well done?"

The lord grinned and scratched his jaw through the thickness of his bright orange beard. A menacing chuckle escaped him as he shifted in his chair and slid a pointed look at the empty seat beside him. "Ye've nay even asked about Lady Christiana. Ye always took quite an interest in her, Commander. Did ye not?"

"It is my hope that the Lady of Argyll is well." He took care to phrase the sentiment in a stilted, detached manner. Last summer, during a sweltering hot, overcrowded feast, he had made the mistake of escorting the fine lady outside for some air before she swooned. Some worrisome fool alerted the MacDougall, and the fiery-tempered man, drunk at the time, had tried to kill him. While there had been no danger of the lord succeeding, fighting the man off without doing him harm proved to be a chore. A fair enough chieftain, the lord paid his warriors well in money, land, and titles. 'Twould be a shame to lose him. "And how are yer children, my liege? How many sons have ye now?"

The MacDougall's eyes narrowed beneath his bushy brows that mirrored the color of his beard. "Three sons. Two daughters. All are well, thank ye."

The hall remained silent as a tomb, air crackling like a building storm. No one moved. Just stood with their tankards held aloft. Even the fire in the main hearth kept quiet as it consumed the stack of mighty logs.

"Since I dinna wish to waste yer valuable time, m'lord, might I ask why ye called me here?" The longer Ross stood on the wide flagstone dubbed the judging stone, the more he wished he had brought along his brothers, Thorburn and Valan. The MacDougall liked Thorburn and tolerated Valan. But three in front of the chieftain were always better than one. "I ken well enough that whilst ye value my warring expertise, ye dinna give a rat's arse about my presence in yer hall."

That won him an amused snort. His liege lifted his hand and snapped his fingers. "Yer reward, Commander Ross."

The guard to the left of the dais rumbled out a hateful chortling, strode to the nearby side door, and yanked it open. With a jerk of his thumb, he motioned for whoever or whatever waited in the alcove to enter the hall.

A half-grown lad stumbled into the room, then whirled and spat at the guard who shoved him along. Long legs and scrawny arms akimbo, he shuffled beneath the weight of the shackles and chains locked around his ankles. Dressed in ragged trews and a threadbare, oversized hauberk that might once have passed for armor, the boy's thin frame pained Ross.

The waif's ratty red hair pulled back in a knobby braid, made his face appear even more gaunt. The child needed a meal. Several, in fact. And worst of all, the poor beggar had a bright red patch staining a good bit of his right cheek. The devil's mark, some would call it. Ross didn't believe in such superstitious nonsense. But he knew such a strange coloring of skin always cursed its bearer. His distant cousin, a sweet lass, had ended her life because of such cruel ridicule.

A corner of the MacDougall's mustache rose, and his eyes twinkled with a devious glint. "As I said, yer reward, Commander. A gift from O'Conor of Connacht."

Ross eyed the youngling, then chose his words with care. "The Earl of Connacht?"

"Aye." The MacDougall nodded. He settled back more comfortably in his ornately carved chair and rested his elbows on its arms. "Ye remember the man. Ye cuckolded him, too."

"I never cuckolded yerself, m'lord," Ross said, addressing the *too* in that statement. "Nor would I."

"Be that as it may, ye did bed O'Conor's wife. Did ye not?"

Ross shifted in place, noting this so-called reward smacked of a public shaming right before an execution. "I also recall saving the man's life. Did he fail to mention that?" He wouldn't deny sharing the lovely Lady Shannon's bed, but his personal code demanded he not brag about it outright.

The MacDougall's beard split with another wicked smile. "Aye. He did mention that. In fact, 'twas why he sent this gift to ye." His smirk slid to the mottle-faced lad who looked ready to either collapse from hunger or burst into a screaming fury.

Not quite certain what to say and sensing the trap had yet to be sprung, Ross gave a polite nod. "While I appreciate the O'Conor's generosity, I must decline the offer of the boy. My two knaves, Tam and Munro, see to my weapons and provisions. I dinna need another, and seeing as how I live in the barracks with my men, I need no servant or slave either."

Laughter rumbled through the hall, making Ross tense and slide his hand to the haft of his sword. "And what do yer grovelers find so amusing, m'lord?"

Still stroking his beard, the MacDougall's focus slid back to the half-grown child. "This is neither knave, slave, nor servant for ye, Commander." His toothy smile, irritating and malicious, returned. "O'Conor sent this gift to be yer life's companion." With a mock frown, he tapped his chin as though struggling to sort through his memories. "What was it the missive said? Ah, yes. That he would do ye the favor of sending ye a helpmate marked by the devil himself. One no other man would ever wish to bed. 'Twill be a proper marriage, indeed." A wicked chuckle rumbled from him. "Said it was the least he could do since ye killed his assassin as well as the one who hired him."

"Marriage? To a boy child?" Ross drew his sword. "This is a damn sorry jest, m'lord."

The boy's jaw tightened, and his gaze jerked downward. Probably in relief, most likely. Poor abused bairn.

"Introduce yerself," the lord barked, tapping his fingertips on his carved armrests in gleeful anticipation.

The waif pulled his defensive stare up from the floor and locked his golden-brown eyes on Ross. "I am Elise O'Cleirigh. Daughter of Lady Cillian. And I will thank ye to know I am a woman grown." She bared her teeth as if bracing for a hurtful response.

A weighty sense of shame bowed Ross's head. It consumed him, burning through his innards like a bitter poisonous bile. This very public humiliation no longer centered on him, but also engulfed this poor lass who had done nothing to deserve it. He knew O'Conor, and he damn well knew the pettiness of the MacDougall. Both men would do anything to soothe their wounded pride. Even if it meant crushing the spirit of a helpless woman.

Outrage shoved aside his shame. Churned hot and fierce within him. He stood taller and strode forward. As gallant as if addressing the queen, he offered the lass a formal bow. "It is my pleasure to meet ye, Lady Elise. Ross MacDougall, at yer service."

The woman didn't so much as flicker an eyelash, but the shadows shifted in the rich whisky hue of her eyes. She didn't speak, just dipped her chin in leery acceptance of his greeting.

"Fetch the scribe," the MacDougall ordered the pair of guards who had brought her forward. His attention returned to Ross. "The papers are ready 'cept for yer mark." He shifted again and puckered a frown at Elise. "If ye canna write yer name, an X will do well enough on the marriage contract."

Her mouth curled into a taunting sneer. "I can read and write as good as anyone. Probably better than most in this hall."

The lord twitched and jerked his focus back to Ross. "Ye would do well to educate yer wife on the proper way to address her liege, ye ken?" He tossed her another glance, then shook his head. "A beating or two would nay be amiss for this one. I'd wager a barrel of my best whisky on that." Eyeing her face, his nose wrinkled as if he smelled a stench. "Best burn some sage and fetch an amulet for protection first though."

The man's cruelty infuriated Ross even more. Women and children were not unruly animals meant to be broken by beatings and public mocking. An honorable warrior protected those weaker than himself. He knew exactly what to do. "I willna sign the marriage contract until we have a proper wedding ceremony in the kirk." He turned to Elise and softened his tone. "And I wouldna recommend ye sign it until after we've stood before the priest. Ye deserve better, Lady Elise."

Both her feathery brows shot higher as if she couldn't believe her ears.

Ross tipped his head toward her shackles. "Free her of her bonds and grant her a room and a maid, so she might prepare herself, ye ken?"

"I suppose ye'll be demanding a gown for her as well?"

"Aye, that would be most appreciated." Ross locked a fierce glare on the MacDougall.

His liege's face flared a darker red, and for the first time since this debacle began, he appeared ill at ease.

Ross didn't try to curb his smile at besting his ill-tempered lord yet again. The man had planned poorly when he dragged an innocent into a weak attempt at public vengeance. "If ye canna arrange all we require by this afternoon, I feel certain tomorrow would do just as well. After all, a proper feast to celebrate a *Gallóglaigh* commander's wedding would nay be amiss. Consider it a gift if ye like." He widened his stance and tapped his fingers atop the pommel of his sword. "Word will spread far and wide of yer generosity, m'lord. 'Twill aid us with recruiting fresh blood in the spring." While he felt his surliness justified, common sense bade him give the Lord of Argyll a bit of leeway. After all, the man possessed powerful connections. Ross didn't fear him, but it paid to taunt the man cautiously.

The MacDougall's cheeks calmed to a less furious shade. "Fair point, Commander." His tone became less menacing. "Ye mentioned ye live in the barracks with yer men?"

"Aye." Ross braced himself. It appeared the MacDougall's game was not at an end.

"Where the hell is that scribe?" The lord turned and fixed a furious glare on the guard remaining by the side door.

"I thought—" The man cut off his excuse, made a curt bow,

and backed away. "I shall fetch him myself, m'lord."

The chieftain snapped his fingers at the other guard standing to the right of the dais. "Remove her bonds."

The man hurried forward and removed the shackles from Elise's wrists and ankles.

"If the two of ye would care to wait in my library, I shall reveal yet another gift once that feckin' scribe is found." The chieftain pushed himself to his feet and swept a hard glare across the room. "We feast tonight to celebrate the marriage of one of my finest *Gallóglaigh*. I would have it known that the Lord of Argyll is a generous man." With a narrow-eyed scowl first at Elise, then at Ross, he made to step down off the dais, then paused and frowned at all those gathered in the hall. "Out of here. Now. All of ye."

The onlookers cleared like mice scattering for the shadows. Before the lord disappeared through a door concealed in the wall behind the dais, he turned and focused on Ross. "Ye won this day, but it isna over yet. To the library with the both of ye."

"Aye, m'lord." Ross held out his arm to Elise. "Come, m'lady." He paused and waited for the guards nearest them to follow the lord. In a lower voice, he continued, "Dealing with Himself is like playing chess. We must think at least three moves ahead at all times. Even more, if possible. 'Tis the best way to survive."

"That man is a swill drinking toad," she murmured, then clamped her lips together as if she hadn't meant to say the words aloud.

Ross cleared his throat to keep from chuckling. With a gentle pat atop her grimy hand, he escorted her to the arch leading to the library. "Ye can always speak yer mind with me," he said softly. "But take care no one else ever overhears, ye ken? At least while we're here at Dunstaffnage."

She nodded, falling back two steps as he opened the door to the library.

Perplexed, he motioned her forward. "M'lady? Ye always

enter first, aye? 'Tis only proper."

As she eyed him, her reddish-blonde brows drew together. "Are ye saying the way ye acted in there will continue until we leave?"

"The way I acted in there?"

"All polite and such. As if I'm not meant to be a slave or a pet."

"Ye're not meant to be a slave. Or a pet." He held out his hand, his earlier apprehension returning. The challenge of helping this woman would not be as easy as he thought. "Come. We will speak more in here. In private."

Her brow smoothed, but her eyes narrowed. A coolness settled across her features. "I understand." She marched into the room, came to a halt in front of the elaborately tiled hearth, and stared down at the fire.

While Ross prided himself on his ability to charm a woman as well as satisfy them in their bedchambers, understanding the complicated creatures proved to be another matter entirely. He closed the door and joined her in front of the hearth. "Even in here, mind yer words," he warned in a low tone. "Especially when close to the tapestries."

She stole a backward glance at the room. "Tapestries cover every wall," she whispered. "I thought libraries held books."

"Not here." He moved to the sideboard covered with bottles, decanters, goblets, and tankards. "Wine, whisky, or ale, m'lady?"

"A whisky would be lovely."

He poured two whiskies, rejoined her at the hearth, and offered her the drink.

She didn't move to take it, just watched as if expecting him to yank it out of her reach. With her attention locked on the golden nectar swirling in the glass, she wet her lips and swallowed hard.

Ross recognized that look from experience with rescuing political prisoners. He set his own drink aside, placed hers in her hand, and curled her fingers around it. "How long since ye last ate?"

"I canna recall." She took the barest sip, then closed her eyes as if savoring the flavor of the burn.

Just as he feared. He strode across the room and yanked hard on the braided rope hanging beside the door. Within moments, a light knock pecked on the other side. He opened it to a young maid who edged back a step as if ready to run at the slightest hint of danger.

"Bring a fine platter of apples, cheese, and bannocks slathered thick with butter. Quick as ye can, lass." He fished a coin from an inner pocket sewn into the waistband of his trews and showed it to her. "Make it extra quick and a groat for ye on yer return, aye?"

The maidservant's eyes flared wide, her gaze focused on the bit of silver. "Aye, m'lord." She bobbed a quick curtsy and took off like an arrow loosed from a bow.

Ross smiled to himself and tucked the coin back inside his waistband. He fetched the bottle of whisky from the sideboard and meandered back to Elise. "Another, m'lady?"

She didn't answer, just stood there hugging the empty glass to her chest.

"M'lady?" He proffered the bottle, leaning the mouth of it toward her cup.

With a twitching start, she blinked rapidly, as though waking from a dream. "Thank ye." She held it out but watched him instead of the glass. "Why did ye do that?"

"Do what?" He had a fair idea what she meant, but it always paid to be certain with women.

"Order food and bribe the maid to get it here with haste." She hazarded another sip.

He noticed she held it on her tongue again, savoring the drink as if fearing she would never get another. "Ye need food, lass. I fear a brisk wind will carry ye away."

"All the better for yerself. Then ye'd not be troubled with a wife such as me." Bitterness rang in her tone as she turned back to the fire and stared down at it. "Ye dinna have to play at being kind. I know ye dinna want anything to do with the likes of me."

"I never play at being kind." He poured her another, then nodded at the glass. "Last one 'til we get some food in ye, aye?" He hazarded a smile. "Ye must be able to stand at the altar."

She gave him a confused squint but didn't comment. Instead, she sipped the drink, eyeing him over the rim of the glass.

Another light knocking at the door broke the strained silence between them.

"Enter."

The maid from earlier pushed the door open, then rolled a cart inside. "All that ye asked for, m'lord, plus a mite extra as there be the two of ye."

Ross pointed at a small, round table beside the window on the other end of the room. "Over there." He fished out the coin he had promised, added another to it, and handed them both to the girl. "Ye seem a bright lass. What be yer name?"

With her attention fixed on the coins, the maidservant dipped another curtsy. "Florie, m'lord."

"Have ye any experience in taking care of a lady?" Ross didn't care that he poached a servant from the MacDougall. The way he figured it, the man owed Elise for such coarse mistreatment. "My betrothed will need a kindhearted lass to see to her needs, starting immediately." He pulled yet another coin from his pocket. "I shall pay ye well as long as ye're honest, dinna gossip, and draw no complaints from yer mistress here. What say ye?"

"Aye, m'lord." Florie stole a glance at Elise, then offered a shy tip of her head. "If the lady finds me suitable, I would think m'self fortunate to be in yer employ."

Ross turned to Elise, who appeared to be as uncertain and wide-eyed as young Florie. "M'lady?"

"What?"

"Does she meet with yer approval for a lady's maid?"

As she edged toward the table bearing the food, Elise gave a leery shrug. "Since I've no idea what a lady's maid does, I wager she'll have an easy enough job of it." Snatching up a bannock, she stuffed as much of it into her mouth as she could shove.

"I shall take that as a *yes*." Ross turned back to the maidservant. "As soon as Himself's finished with us in here, my lady shall need yer help in preparing for our wedding."

"I'll order the water heated for her bath now, m'lord." Florie aimed a curtsy at Elise, dipped another at Ross, then scurried out the door.

A sense of satisfaction filled Ross as he watched the girl go. An outburst of coughing snapped his attention back to Elise. Her face an alarming shade of red, she thumped her chest and clutched at her throat. Ross rushed forward and filled a tankard with water from the pitcher Florie had brought along with the food. "Slow down, lass. I swear ye will never go hungry again. Not as long as I draw breath."

"Ye say that," she wheezed out between sips of water. She plunked the tankard back on the table, then leaned against it as she continued coughing and gasping for air.

He refrained from arguing or assuring her she could trust him. Nay. It would do no good to speak of trust with this one. All the scarring from her past demanded she experience kindness firsthand until she believed it wasn't some cruel trick to deceive her. He fetched a chair and helped her sit. "Rest and eat. Himself will join us soon. He acted as though he had more to reveal."

She snorted out a bitter laugh, took another swig of water, then shoved a sizable chunk of cheese into her mouth. "Then I shall strive to enjoy what verra well might be my last meal."

Even though he didn't want a wife and had no idea what to do with one, Ross vowed to make Elise's life better, so she might heal. If he helped this woman regain her strength and escape her past, mayhap it would wipe away some of the marks he'd made on own his soul. He needed all the help he could get to erase a few of those stains.

The library door burst open, admitting the Lord of Argyll and a wisp of a man that Ross assumed must be the latest scribe. His liege went through scribes faster than grass through a goose. The man's erratic temperament drove them away. With a self-important strut, the chieftain made his way to the massive mahogany desk in the corner.

"Show him," he ordered the scribe.

"I told ye neither of us will sign the marriage papers 'til we've stood before the priest." Ross wouldn't put anything past the MacDougall.

"Already come to an accord, have ye?" The pompous man pursed his lips and hooked his thumbs in his belt. "Good. Man and wife should always agree." His tone belied his words.

"If ye would come to the desk, m'lord," the scrawny man said with a wave of the rolled parchment. "Himself bade me draw up this title. Ye will find the solicitor's mark already on the document, as well. All neat and tidy, it is. He said he would come and speak with ye if ye had questions." The scribe leaned closer and lowered his voice to a whisper. "With one of his women right now, ye understand, and refuses to be interrupted." He tapped on the parchment again and his voice returned to a normal tone. "Just needs signing and then we'll send a copy to Edinburgh for proper recording."

"Title to what?" Ross didn't trust the MacDougall any farther than he could throw him, and the man had increased in girth since the last time they'd met.

"To yer new keep, Commander." The slyness of the lord's smile eroded Ross's trust even more. *"Tùr Singilte."*

Ross knew of the place. A lone broch that lay almost at the halfway point between Dunstaffnage and his brother Thorburn's castle, Dunthoradelle. "That tower's naught but a pile of rubble."

The MacDougall held up a hand and shook his head. "Nay, 'tis a tower, part of a skirting wall, and several buildings within." With a slight shrug, he added, "It does need a few repairs, but this document states that anything ye require to restore the place shall be provided by Dunstaffnage."

"Will it now?" Ross refrained from telling the man he was so full of shite he stank. "All the supplies we need, and they'll nay cost us so much as a pence?"

"All the place shall cost ye is the sweat of yer brow," his liege reassured, with the smoothness of an adder hypnotizing a bird. "In fact, I feel so generous, I shall even send a few men to help with the repairs until all are completed." He waved away the scribe. "Leave the document for the commander's review, whilst ye fetch us a pair of witnesses."

"Aye, m'lord." The wee man skittered from the room and softly closed the door behind him.

"Why would ye offer such?" Ross stood between the Mac-Dougall and Elise, blocking her from his view so she might finish her meal with no further untoward comments. He wanted the Lord of Argyll focused solely on himself. "Ye've always paid me well, but this level of generosity smacks of an unsavoriness I prefer not to speak of. At what cost is this benevolence?"

The lord lowered himself into the chair behind the desk. He nodded toward the decanters. "Pour us a whisky, aye?"

Ross hesitated, reluctant to open the chieftain's view to the far end of the room where Elise sat at the table.

"I willna torment yer woman further," the MacDougall promised in a resigned tone. "Lady Christiana stood behind the servant screen and viewed our earlier, more public, meeting. I spied her, but too late to save my arse. 'Tis why I ended our conversation and had ye come in here. My lady wife was less than pleased with my behavior." His demeanor softened, losing all malice. "But before ye grant yerself too much importance, know that it was the mistreatment of the lass—not the baiting of yer ire that stirred her rage. She kens well enough how ye use women and doesna approve." He leaned back in his chair and clasped his hands behind his head. "Ye are correct about *Tùr Singilte*. 'Tis a tumbled-down piece of shite. But I swore to my Christiana to make it right by ye. Whatever ye need, ye shall have."

Ross had always believed Lady Christiana controlled the MacDougall, but he never truly knew for certain until now. God help them all if the woman ever left the man or died before he did. "Then I shall gladly accept yer generosity. I would also ask ye to convey my thanks to the gracious Lady Christiana."

"She is my fiercest conscience, man. Pray to God such a thing never happens to yerself." He rose and nodded toward the decanters again. "Whisky, Commander Ross. Fetch it whilst I summon the scribe and witnesses, aye?"

"Aye, m'lord." As he poured the drinks, Ross stole a sideways glance at Elise. The poor lass hunched over her food like a starving hound guarding a bone. He tried to reassure her with a smile, but she glared at him and continued stuffing leftover crusts, cheese rinds, and pieces of fruit in the folds of her ragged clothing.

The Lord of Argyll returned to his desk with the scribe and a pair of guards in tow. As soon as Ross handed him the glass, he lifted it high. "Do we have an accord, Commander Ross? A wedding, a feast, and a home made fit and fine again, aye?"

"Aye, m'lord. Yer generosity shall be made known to one and all. We most certainly have an accord." He downed his drink, thumped the glass onto the desk, and took the quill from the scribe. "Where do I sign?"

"Right here, Commander." The scribe tapped on the parchment. He cleared his throat, cast a furtive glance at the MacDougall, then tapped a second line on the agreement. "Lady Christiana demands the estate be in the name of the lady as well." He turned and squinted in Elise's direction. "Her mark is needed here."

"M'lady?" Ross held his breath to keep from smiling.

Elise froze mid-bite of a large red apple. As soon as she realized all eyes focused on her, she wiped her mouth with the back of her hand and shoved the rest of the uneaten fruit down the front of her hauberk. She rose from the chair with one arm clutched across her middle to keep her hoard tucked inside her tunic.

Ross's heart ached at the hunger and suffering that trained her to behave in such a way. "Before she signs and all is witnessed, we will also need the larders and root cellars well-stocked for the winter. After all, this is September, ye ken?"

The MacDougall's eyes flexed as though he had just been slapped.

"I feel certain Lady Christiana would agree," Ross added with a wink.

"So be it," the lord growled, nodding at the scribe to add the request to the bottom of the document.

"Initial here, Commander," the tiny man requested.

"Where do I sign?" Elise asked.

"One more thing," Ross interrupted.

"Now what?" the MacDougall growled.

"The estate shall no longer be known as *Túr Singilte*. I wish it christened Tórrelise." He smiled down at the wide-eyed lass still hugging the food stuffed inside her clothing. "Tower of Elise, ye ken?"

The Lord of Argyll rolled his eyes, then nodded at the scribe. "Make it so, then get on with the signing. I weary of this and would have it done and behind me."

The scribe scratched out the words, Elise signed, Ross initialed, and the Tower of Elise came to be.

CHAPTER TWO

E LISE'S STOMACH CLENCHED and growled. The sharp pains almost doubled her over. Such an abundance of food in her belly confused it, becoming nearly as painful as having nothing in it at all. She swallowed hard and hugged her confiscated scraps tighter. While she might be full as a fattened calf now, who knew when she might eat again? These Scots could be toying with her, making her believe kindness existed in these walls just so they could snatch everything away and laugh.

"This way, m'lady." Florie waited a few steps ahead, her expectant smile lit by the torches flickering in the hallway. "It's not all that much farther to the room Himself said would be yers and the commander's 'til tomorrow."

Elise eased forward, watching for whatever evil trick lurked in the shadowy doorways. She'd seen firsthand how the Lord of Argyll treated others for his own amusement. That conniving toad would do anything.

"What happens tomorrow?" she asked as she darted past a shallow alcove containing nothing more than a cross on the wall and a bench for prayerful reflection.

The maidservant bubbled with a joyful giggle as she unlocked the door in the next alcove. "We all leave for yer new home, of course. For Tórrelise." Chin tucked to her shoulder, she offered a shy smile. "Such a fine name, m'lady. So romantic for the commander to name it for yerself."

"I suppose." Elise followed Florie into a room so opulent it had to be a mistake. Pillowed chairs and cushioned benches. A roaring fire in the hearth with a pair of multi-branched candelabras flickering on the mantle. Every wall displayed large, colorful tapestries, perfect for keeping out winter's chill. Floor weaves so thick, she had to pick up her feet lest she stumble across the padded coverings. "Are ye certain we should be in here? This canna be the right room."

"Course it is, m'lady. This is the room for yerself and the commander." The girl stole another glance at her. The sympathetic quirk to the maid's mouth stung like a slap in the face.

"Do not pity me!" Elise spun away from the girl. She marched to a table deep in a shadowy corner and placed her stash of food in a neat pile, then covered it with an embroidered linen she snatched from a nearby nightstand. With a stern look back, she held her head high. "If ye pity me, I shall tell that Scot to leave ye here, and ye can keep serving that toad of a chieftain."

"Beg pardon, m'lady. I meant ye no harm or cruelty." Florie lowered her gaze. Without looking up, she clasped her hands and twitched the slightest shrug. "I dinna pity ye, m'lady. Yer courage is braw because 'tis more than a little obvious yer path has nay been an easy one. I wish to help if ye'll but allow it. Please. I mean ye no harm."

A fluttering of guilt gave Elise pause. Perhaps this maidservant was not the enemy. At least, she didn't appear to be *yet*. "What was yer name again?"

"Florie, m'lady." The lass stole a sideways peek up at Elise without lifting her head and offered another smile. "Florie Campbell." As she sidled toward a tall wardrobe, her smile grew, plumping her dimpled cheeks even more. "And I have the most wonderful surprise for ye, m'lady. Lady Christiana not only sent ye a lovely gown for today but also a proper set of clothes to take with ye. Two fine linen shifts. Two kirtles and overdresses with matching aprons and a kertch. Stockings—two pairs of those as well. A braided belt with slippers dyed the same color. A pair of boots. Fine surcoat and a lovely cloak." She opened the doors to the wardrobe and pointed. "Cast yer eyes on all of it, m'lady. Is it not grand for her to have gathered such bounty so quickly?"

Elise wanted to believe this kindness to be real, but she feared it wasn't. She gave Florie a nod and turned away. Everything had gone from bad to worse after Mama died. Shame filled her at the blackness encrusting her nails and the months of grime ground into her skin. Father had banished her from entering his presence. Said it was her devil's mark that killed Mama. His drinking got worse, turning him into a raving madman everyone feared.

When he went away, peace reigned for a little while, but that ended when he returned with a new wife. That vile, wicked woman despised her, too. Sold her to the Earl of Craevan with some ridiculous lie. And after the first night as wife to that man, Elise realized the only way she'd be saved was if she saved herself. Then, while on the run, she'd been captured and become a slave to the Earl of Connacht. Fate hated her and punished her at every turn.

"M'lady?"

"What?" She jerked with a startled twitch and hid her hands behind her back.

"Yer bath is ready in the anteroom." Florie eased forward as if trying to coax a frightened animal into the open. "I perfumed the water with oil of rose. It smells lovely."

"A bath?" After such a long time without a way to wash, she learned to ignore her own stench. But now, the prospect of a bath thrilled her more than if someone handed her a bag of gold. "With heated water? And soap for lathering?"

"Aye, m'lady. If ye will allow it, I'll unbind yer hair, so we can wash it." Florie came to a halt, waiting for permission to come closer.

Wash her hair. Elise felt the burn of joyous tears but blinked hard and fast to stop them. Nay. She must not show how much all this meant to her. That would make them enjoy it all the more when they snatched it away.

"May I, m'lady?" Her plump little fingers twitching, Florie held herself back but looked to be struggling with maintaining control.

"Aye," Elise whispered, praying this wasn't another cruel jest. Time and time again she'd experienced how the simplest of comforts could become as fleeting as a precious dream.

Florie moved behind her and worked at untangling her filthy hair. "Forgive me, m'lady. I dinna mean to pull it."

"It's nay yer fault." Elise welcomed the tugs and yanks. "Do what ye must. I know it to be a rat's nest. Think we shall have to cut it?"

"Nay, m'lady. I'll get it." After a few more yanks, Florie stepped aside. "There now. That's done." She bustled past her, opened the narrow door to the anteroom wider, and waved her forward. "It's lovely warm in here 'cause of the water, but I'll leave the door open for the heat from the fire, too, whilst ye undress." A worried crease drew the girl's dark brows together. "As a lady's maid, am I supposed to undress ye as well as dress ye?"

"I have no idea." Even as wife to the Earl of Craevan, Elise had not had a lady's maid or any maid for that matter. If floors needed scrubbing or meals cooked, she did it. Her husband's money went to brothels, drink, and any other way he found to waste it. None was left to keep any servants other than those forced to stay and work off their debts to the earl. "I can undress m'self if ye need to do other things."

Florie swept her with a sharp-eyed look, starting at her toes and rising to the top of her head. After a moment, she nodded. "Undress yerself, and I'll toss those things in the fire whilst ye bathe. I dinna think they'll bear the hard scrubbing they need. Do ye feel they will?"

"Probably not." As Elise stripped the hauberk off over her head, the material ripped as if to confirm it. After kicking off the last of her garb, she scooped up the pile and started toward the hearth. "I'll put them on the fire. I dinna wish ye offended by the filth."

"Ye havena seen filth until ye've helped raise five younger brothers." Florie grabbed the clothes, then nodded toward the steaming tub. "Take yer ease, m'lady. I lined the barrel with a double layer of linen so the metal wouldna be so harsh against ye. Do ye wish to wear a shift whilst ye bathe? Ye're mighty thin, if ye pardon my saying so."

"Thank ye, but I wish to scrub every inch of myself until I can see my freckles." She stepped into the hot water and groaned. She couldn't help it. The heat seeped into her bones and soothed her in a way she couldn't put into words. After a deep breath, she sank below the surface, wishing she could stay there forever. By the time she came up for air, Florie had returned with her sleeves rolled up to her elbows.

"Ready to find those freckles, m'lady?" The cheerful maid held up a crock overflowing with a creamy white substance that smelled as sweet as a field of flowers. "Or hair first?"

"Hair, I think." Elise closed her eyes as Florie soaped, scrubbed, then soused her and did it all over again until the water cooled and turned a dingy gray. When she stepped from the tub, she felt a full stone lighter. Wrapped in a double length of linen, she short-stepped her way to the hearth, basking in its warmth as Florie combed out her hair.

"Ye've the prettiest hair, m'lady." The girl cast a glance at the door, then grinned. "Not the color of a pumpkin like Himself's, but pretty like a red deer's coat."

A banging on the door made them both jump. "All are ready and waiting in the kirk," a deep voice called out. "Himself said to make haste, ye ken?"

"I canna believe they expect a lady to prepare in the blink of an eye." Florie stormed over to the door, her roundish form moving with the speed of a charging bull. She yanked it open a crack and aimed a stern finger at whoever stood on the other side. "'Twill be at least a little while longer. My mistress doesna wish to disappoint her betrothed."

"Himself said—"

"I heard ye the first time ye said it." She shut the door with a firm thud before the man could say another word. Eyes sparkling and cheeks rosy with excitement, Florie marched back and resumed her combing of Elise's hair.

"Ye're nay afraid they'll beat ye? Or starve ye?" Elise winced as the maid yanked through a stubborn snarl. Her captor had used those tactics on his servants.

"Lady Christiana would never allow such a thing." Florie massaged lotions and oils all over Elise until her skin glowed. "And Commander Ross isna a cruel man from all I've heard tell about him." She held a chemise ready to slip over Elise's head. "But ye ken he told me I mustn't gossip."

Slipping the garment on, Elise shook it down. She winced as her calloused hands snagged in the soft, fine weave of the linen. Thankfully, Florie had trimmed away her filthy, broken nails, but the roughness of her palms could nay be helped. She forced aside the regret and forged onward with the search for information.

"The commander also told ye I must never complain about ye." That should get the girl talking. "So, be a lamb and tell me everything ye know about the man. After all, he is to be my husband." She would rather go into this prepared.

"First the kirtle, then the overdress." Florie spoke with the tone of a mother reminding a child to be patient. "'Tis such a pretty gown, m'lady. The deep green suits ye."

Elise complied without argument, but only because the heightened color on the maid's face revealed she was eager to tell all she knew. As the lass smoothed and buttoned the long, fitted sleeves, Elise prodded her again. "Tell me, Florie. For my sake. I beg ye."

Florie's eyes sparkled as she continued buttoning and lacing. "All the women love him and hope he'll look their way. All the men hate him whilst, at the same time, wish they were him." Her voice grew hushed. "He is a mighty warrior, proven himself in many a campaign, and rumored to be just as artful at bed play as he is with his weapons."

"How does he treat his servants? His slaves?"

"I dinna ken." Florie paused, looking as though the question befuddled her to a full stop. "His knaves are proud to serve him. Other than that, I dinna think he has any servants." Her perpetual grin blossomed into a bigger smile. "I guess I am one of the first. Is that not grand?"

Elise liked the maid but decided the girl's bubbly nature could be exhausting. "Yes, Florie. Grand, indeed."

"And now the fine surcoat, and then I'll show ye the way to the kirk." The maid's voice trembled with awe as she held up the sumptuous garment for Elise to slip her arms through. "Velvet lined with fur, m'lady. Lady Christiana insisted ye must have it for the warmth alone since ye've no fat on yer bones to get ye through the winter."

"This is as fine as the one my mother had." Elise rubbed her hands across the rich burgundy softness. "Why would the lady be so kind and generous to me? I've never met the woman." More of what Florie said came to the forefront of her mind. "And how does she know I am thin? She's never laid eyes on me near as I can tell."

"Lady Christiana knows everything that goes on within this keep." Florie urged her toward the door. "She is a woman of faith and kind as she can be. All here consider themselves blessed to serve her."

Partway out the door, Elise paused. "And now ye've been pulled away from such a fine mistress and saddled with me." Poor trusting maid. She had no idea what a terrible turn her luck had taken. "I am cursed, Florie, and so sorry that ye're now damned along with me."

"I always heard tell the Irish were more superstitious than us." Florie shooed her down the hallway as if she were a goose. "Dinna misunderstand," she advised as she straightened the folds of Elise's skirts as they walked. "We Scots are a superstitious people, as well, but I believe we all have the power to make our own fate, ye ken?"

"Make our own fate?"

"Aye." The girl dipped her chin with such certainty that her dark curls quivered. "Grab yer fate by the bollocks and dinna let go until it does what ye wish."

A snorting laugh bubbled free of Elise, startling her so much, she came to a halt.

"What is it, m'lady?" Florie paused just as she pulled open the large arched door to the courtyard.

"You made me laugh." Elise pressed a hand to her chest, cherishing the return of the lighthearted warmth. "I've not laughed in an age or longer."

Florie gave a polite tip of her head. "I am glad, m'lady. Mam always said I was put on this earth to spread happiness. God willing, I'll do what I can to help ye grab yer fate by the bollocks and make it stop being such an arse to ye."

The faintest flickering of hope sparked deep within Elise's core. It felt strange and too wonderful to trust. Hope had left her a long time ago, but now it was back again, whispering in her ear.

"Come, m'lady." Florie urged her through the door and pointed at the path that passed through an arched opening in the outer wall. "That path will take ye straight to the kirk."

"Ye'll not be coming with me?" She'd faced many frightening things, but the thought of walking into that chapel alone disquieted her.

"Ye wish me to?"

"Yes, Florie. Please come." She plucked at the surcoat, pulling it closer. The heavy, fur-lined velvet blocked the brisk autumn wind cutting across the grounds but didn't help a bit with the icy touch of the unknown.

Florie looped her arm through hers. "I'll be happy to show ye the way, m'lady."

They followed the path in silence. Even the sea crashing against the shore seemed muted. The closer they got to the small church of carved stones, the drier Elise's mouth became. Heaven help her, she wondered if this priest would accept a nod in place of an *I do*. Lord Craevan's holy man had done so since she stood before him bound and gagged. At least here, the Lady of Argyll and Ross insisted on kindness and respect. Or at least, they did for now.

Head held high, she forced herself to slow her breathing. She'd nay act the coward. With her hands clasped against her churning middle, she climbed the steps.

Florie urged her onward with a smile and a nod. As Elise stepped inside, the sight of her intended waiting at the altar weakened her ability to maintain an aloof air. Back in the hall, with his pummeled face and muscular bulk, he had looked like the monster she heard all *Gallóglaigh* warriors to be. But now, Commander Ross presented a handsome figure of power that made the tales of women fawning at his feet quite easy to believe.

Even with one of his eyes still swelled shut, his face shone, freshly washed. His combed hair reflected candlelight like newly minted gold. Hard, rugged, and handsome he was, with his closely trimmed beard and squared jaw. His short whiskers shimmered as bronze as a field of wheat ready for harvest except for a narrow strip of the whitest white running up the center of his chin. That stripe pointed to the bow of his fine, full lips as if a woman might need help to aim her kiss.

He had the eyes of a falcon, sharp and piercing, at least the one that was open. With his muscular frame garbed in a regal hauberk and fur-lined surcoat, the man looked like a mighty god-king either descended from Heaven or risen from Hell itself. The sword belted at his waist looked as long as she was tall and probably weighed three times as much. If he possessed the power to swing such a weapon, what else might he be able to do?

She sent up a silent prayer for cunning, strength, and fearless-ness. To survive this man would require a hearty dose of all three and then some. Then he smiled at her, and the split in his puffy lip glistened with fresh blood. At least she wouldn't have to worry about kisses. With some surprise, a sad dip of disappointment made her swallow hard at that realization. Bitterness mocked her for the foolishness of such thoughts. No man like him would ever wish to kiss her. She embraced the painful truth and held it close as she forced herself up the aisle. The mark on her face had saved her many a time. She thanked God above she had never been saddled with the slightest beauty.

"M'lady." He extended his hand, seeming not to realize that the deep rumble of his voice held the magic of a lover's caress. Or at least, she assumed so, having never experienced such a thing.

She slid her hand into his, thankful that Florie had scrubbed away the filth and trimmed her nails.

"Ye are loveliness itself, Lady Elise," he whispered, his words meant for her alone.

He confused her with such foolish talk. The man didn't wish to be married. Kindness was one thing but taking on the burden of a wife was quite another. Why bother to say such things when they weren't the truth? She frowned up at him, trying to get a better understanding of what slyness he played. The shadows flitting through the stormy blue of his uninjured eye appeared unfathomable.

When she failed to respond, his pale brows twitched downward into a befuddled slant. But he didn't comment, merely gave her a polite bow, then turned them to face the priest.

"Welcome, my children," the holy man began, his whining voice grating on Elise's already raw sensibilities. She didn't trust priests. The last one, Craevan's bought-and-paid-for man, had foiled one of her attempts at escape—all for a barrel of cheap wine.

The father cleared his throat and stared at her. Apparently, the man had asked her a question.

"What?" She would not offer him any special politeness. This man of God was probably as corrupt as the last one.

"Yer name, child?" He leaned closer and raised his voice as though he thought her deaf. "What is yer full Christian name?"

"Elise O'Cleirigh," she shouted back. "And I'm nay deaf. I was merely lost in my thoughts and didna hear what ye said."

Her ill-fated husband-to-be snorted a laugh, then clamped a fist against his mouth in a futile attempt at staunching his amusement.

The priest fixed him with a dark look, thumped his open prayerbook, then cleared his throat again. "Do ye, Ross MacDougall, take Elise O'Cleirigh to be yer wife, swearing to protect her no matter what life lays at yer door until death takes ye from her side?"

Ross cleared his throat and stood taller. "I do."

The holy man turned back to her, started to lean closer, then stopped himself. "Do ye, Elise O'Cleirigh, take Ross MacDougall to be yer husband, swearing to bear his children, submit and serve him no matter what life brings to yer door until death relieves ye from this sacred duty?"

"Since I have no choice, I suppose I must."

"Ungrateful wench," the Lord of Argyll growled from his station on the other side of Ross.

Out of the corner of her eye, Elise noticed Florie looked ready to faint dead away. Perhaps she should not speak so brashly. After all, Ross had been kind. "Forgive me, Father. Yes. I take Ross MacDougall as husband and swear to serve him as best I can."

The priest shook his head and blew out a long-suffering sigh. "Then I now pronounce the two of ye man and wife. Let no man tear asunder that which God himself hath joined." He snapped the prayer book shut and tipped it toward them. "Ye may kiss."

Elise pulled in a deep breath and held it as she turned toward her new husband. He shocked her when he slid a finger under her chin, tipped up her face, and brushed the gentlest of kisses across her mouth. So tender. Almost as if he cared about whether or not she felt at ease. She scolded herself. Such a fool she was. The man's split lip pained him. How else would he kiss?

As he drew away, he smiled down at her, then placed her hand in the crook of his arm and led her up the altar steps to the table containing their marriage agreement. He signed his name, then handed the quill to her.

She inked the nib, then paused above the line beside his. Whether or not she signed, this marriage would not be legal. After all, since Lord Craevan still lived, she was his wife even though the marriage had never been consummated. An annulment could be gotten, but why bother? No one cared, and come spring, she would escape this second husband and be free at last. And this escape would be more successful. She had learned much from her mistakes in Ireland. With a firm stroke, she signed her name.

"Well done." Ross offered his arm again. "Shall we stroll down to the sea so it might bless our union?"

"As ye wish, m'lord." She cringed at the words as soon as she said them. The barbaric Earl of Connacht had demanded that response from all servants in his household or a beating followed. Once she escaped, she had sworn not to utter that phrase again. But old habits beaten into a body died hard.

"We dinna have to walk the grounds if ye dinna wish it." Ross came to a halt and stared down at her with the faintest puckering of his handsome brow. "Speak yer mind, lass. Just because they bridled ye with my name doesna mean ye must go wherever I lead."

"A walk will be nice," she said, still struggling to understand this hulking beast of a man. No matter what Florie said, Commander Ross couldn't be this kind and considerate. Especially not to her.

"We will return in time for the feast," Ross announced to those following them out of the chapel.

The lady walking beside the Lord of Argyll smiled and gave an approving nod. The toady man himself shrugged as if he couldn't care less. Florie looked ecstatic, but the maid always appeared overjoyed.

"I wished for us to walk together, so I might apologize," he said quietly, squinting as he stared across the waves glittering beneath the sun.

"Apologize?" She watched him, half expecting to be tossed into the sea so the tide might carry her away.

"For the cruelty of their jest." He kept his gaze locked on the horizon. "I deserve their spite." He slowly turned and faced her, a pained tenseness flexing his jaw. "Ye dinna deserve such coarse treatment because of me."

"I see." What else could she say? What if this was a trap? Another cruel game?

"I will take care of ye, m'lady. I am not a rich man, but I'm far from poor. I swear ye shall want for nothing."

"Why?"

"Why?" The befuddled furrow returned to his brow, deeper this time.

"Why do ye care if I live or die?" She eased a step back, in case her question angered him. It always paid to have room to dodge a strike.

"Because when they chose to saddle ye with my name, ye became my responsibility." His firm but calm tone confused her even more. He gave her a lopsided grin. "I never shirk a responsibility."

When he reached for her, she ducked behind her arm and braced for the strike. 'Twas the best she could do in this gown. In these skirts, she could never outmaneuver him.

"M'lady?"

She peeped over her raised arm, curious at the hurt echoing in his tone. A trap. His astonishment and dismay had to be a trap.

But he didn't move, just stared at her, a sad weariness aging him. "I will never strike ye, Elise. No matter what ye say or do."

"Never is a long time, m'lord." Slowly, she lowered her arm and smoothed her hands down the velvety surcoat.

"I will never give ye reason to fear me." He moved away from her, putting an arm's length of space between them as he clasped his hands behind his back. "As I said before, ye will never want for anything." He pulled in a deep breath and released it with a heavy sigh. "And as God is my witness, I will never touch ye if ye dinna wish it. Do ye understand my meaning?"

"I am not a fool," she said quietly but amended her tone so as not to sound so shrewish. He didn't wish to touch her because of her face. It had saved her from unwanted advances before. "But will yer boar of a liege not demand a witness to the consummation?"

"What happens in my bedchamber is no one's affair but mine." Ross resettled his stance. "Even though I ordered yer maid not to gossip, I am quite certain she told ye of my reputation. Did she not?"

"I have no complaints about Florie." She didn't wish to get the maid in trouble. After all, she had asked the girl for the information.

He gave her a sad grin, scrubbed a hand down his face, then winced as he hit his sore eye. "I dinna strike maids either, m'lady. Women are meant to be cherished and protected, no matter their station in life. Not beaten. Not ravaged. Not abused in any way."

She didn't wish to anger him, but she wasn't about to act like a mindless fool and follow along with anything he said. "Those are strange words for a *Gallóglaigh*."

"Not for this *Gallóglaigh*. Nor my brothers." He offered his arm again. "Shall we go inside? This wind is colder than I realized, and I fear ye may take a chill." He stood with his arm extended, waiting for her to come to him. "We shall find a bit of whisky and sit by the fire until the feast. Would that be pleasing to ye?"

"Yes. Thank ye." She took his arm, confused to the core about this odd man she had just married.

CHAPTER THREE

S O, HE HAD a wife. Now what? He knew how to treat other men's wives but had never planned on having one of his own.

Ross rubbed his nape, somehow reliving a sharp cuff to the back of his head. The sort Mother always gave when he tested her patience one time too many. He stole a sideways glance at the wisp of a lass walking beside him. The grubby waif he had thought was a lad had disappeared. Who knew that beneath all the filth and rags hid an intriguing fae-like lass as delicate and lovely as morning mist dancing across the heather?

He clenched his teeth at the memory of her cowering. How could anyone strike such a woman? And yet they had. She acted like a feral animal, caged and beaten until she no longer cared what it might take to escape her pain.

While he had no use for a wife, he would see her happy. Content with the best he could give her. And by all that was holy, he would see her fed until the hollows of her cheeks and those sunken eyes disappeared. A mighty warrior he might be, but never could he stomach the suffering of an innocent, whether it be a woman, child, or animal. His brothers were the same. They all suffered from this softness of the heart because of how their mother and little sister had died. He flinched at the horrific memory's attempt at resurfacing and forced it back into the dark recesses of his mind.

He pulled out Elise's chair and helped her sit, noting how she watched him as if unable to believe he treated her with respect. With a flick of his hand, he flagged a servant bearing two pitchers. "Wine or port, m'lady?"

"Wine or port?" she repeated, her face still flushed from the whisky they enjoyed earlier by the fire.

"Whichever ye wish. Wine or port." He leaned closer so no one else could hear. "Dinna worry. They always bring the bannocks and cheese out first whilst they're pulling apart the meat to bring to the tables. We shall eat a fine meal soon."

Her brow furrowed, then smoothed. "Wine would be grand, thank ye."

"Wine it is." He nodded to the lad with the pitchers. Once her goblet was filled, he lifted his own. "A private toast, aye?"

With a hardened jaw, her eyes flexed into leery slits. She lifted her goblet as well as her chin.

He recognized defiance and fight still alive within her and was glad. "To friendship," he whispered with a touch of his glass to hers.

"Friendship," she repeated, watching him over the rim as she sipped.

As foreseen, maidservants and lads marched through the archway with boards piled high with breads, cheeses, and sliced fruit. They served the head table first, then provided more of the same to the parallel rows of tables running down both sides of the room. His lordship's dogs trotted in, strategically placing themselves behind the tables to garner the best scraps. Servants with a pitcher in each hand meandered up and down the center of the room, ensuring cups and tankards stayed full.

Torches flickered and hissed on either side of the hearth and at equal distances along the walls. Fresh rushes covered the floor, but their usual quiet rustling disappeared beneath the loud hum of conversation. Ross tilted his head, noting the faint howl of the wind outside the stronghold's thick walls.

"First squall of the season," he observed more to himself than anyone else. He searched for a way to speak to his new wife without making her think he was trying to trap her in a lie or planned to beat her. He hated that leeriness in her eyes but wasn't sure how to ease her fears. "Hear the wind?"

"We shall have snow come morning," she said before shoving an entire slice of apple into her mouth and slipping two more into a pouch fastened inside her surcoat.

He blew out a heavy sigh, knowing full well why she did it. "Ye dinna have to do that, ye ken? Not anymore."

"Do what?" she mumbled, her cheeks bulging with food. She made her eyes go wide with feigned innocence, but he saw it for the act that it was.

"I willna keep food from ye. Ye can eat whenever and however much ye wish. I swear it."

Her cheeks flushed a brighter pink, but she held her head high. "Forgive me for shaming ye, m'lord."

"Ye didna shame me." He piled more fruit, cheese, and bread on the trencher in front of her. "Ye make my heart hurt because I wish ye had never known the pain that makes ye behave so."

She eyed him as if she thought him strange, then tossed a glance at the tables running from the dais all the way to the main door. "Do ye not see how they gloat when they look at ye? All because of me." Her eyes narrowed again, and her mouth tightened as if daring him to strike her. "Ye must hate me. If they hadna forced me upon ye, ye wouldna be mocked in such a way."

"Oh, they wouldha found other ways to mock me." He chuckled and selected the choicest bits of meat from the platter the servant presented. With a reassuring wink, he added them to her end of the trencher. "And I dinna give a rat's arse about them or what they think of me." Offering her his eating knife, he continued, "I have my brothers and loyal friends I can trust with my life." To ease her mind and hopefully smooth her defensive bristling, he added, "And now I have a wife who I intend to treat as the lady she is, so she might someday trust me, too."

She didn't comment but stole another side-eyed look at him and continued eating.

Good. She needed to eat. He dreaded what lay ahead and decided that if she wished, he would sleep on the floor or anywhere other than their bed. As guarded as she behaved, he couldn't imagine how strained their wedding night would be.

A pair of servants appeared beside them, one bearing a large bowl and the other holding the fancy bronze ewer that signaled their time in the dining hall had ended, and the washing of hands should begin.

Ross leaned forward and glared down the table, pinning the Lord of Argyll with a threatening scowl. How dare his liege order such a thing done to rush them off to the bedchamber.

The MacDougall answered with a calculating nod and lifted his glass.

The sound of splashing water made him turn back. Her expression cold and blank, Elise sat ramrod straight as the maidservant poured water over her hands and then offered her a clean linen to dry them.

"If ye are nay finished with yer meal, we willna go." He leaned closer and forced her to look him in the eyes. "What do ye wish to do, m'lady?"

"I am fine, m'lord." She dried her hands, then placed the cloth on the table. "I think it best we go. This company of toads has wearied me."

So, a remnant of fire still sparked within the lady. Good. The shadow of a wry smile on her lips encouraged him even more. "I agree, m'lady. Let us be done with the lot of them." He cleaned his hands but stopped the maid with the ewer before she drew away. "I want breads, cheeses, fruits, and all the wine ye can carry brought to my room, ye ken? Ensure a good amount of whisky is brought, too. If the room doesna have any decanters, bring the keg and glasses."

"Aye, Commander." The lass dipped a quick curtsy and hurried away.

He rose and offered Elise his hand, taking care to give his back to the MacDougall, a subtle yet blatant insult he hoped would be noticed by all. The man might be a powerful bastard, but Ross had allowed him all the latitude he would give. It hadn't been that long since his eldest brother forced the Lord of Argyll to back down by threatening to leave and take the mighty *Gallóglaigh* troops with him. Perhaps the man needed reminding again. The MacDougall might be lord over all he could see, but he would not defend nor keep it long without his warriors.

Elise slid her hand into his and stood. She paused and placed the small amount of food she had hoarded back on the table. After a long stare at the pile, she lifted her head and gave him a determined nod. "I am ready, m'lord."

Without a word to anyone, he helped her step down from the dais. All in the room could go straight to hell as far as he cared. Except for the Lady Christiana. Only she had shown genuine kindness to Elise. But if he attempted a bow in her direction, the MacDougall would perceive it as meant for him. So, he strode onward toward the stairwell with his lady on his arm.

The narrow turret staircase prevented them from walking abreast. Ross stepped back and motioned for Elise to take the lead. She didn't speak as she climbed, but her fingers trembled as her pale hand slid along the wall. Once they reached the room, he would ease her mind.

Her steps slowed as they came to the hallway. She lagged back, darting sideways glances at him, then looking straight ahead once more. The wind howled louder, blasting hard against the outer walls as if trying to knock the stones from their foundation.

"'Tis a wicked night," he said as he pushed open the door and stepped aside to allow her first entry.

She answered with a tense smile, bowed her head, and hurried into the room. Once she reached the hearth, she came to a halt and stared down at the fire, stretching out her hands toward the warmth. Its glow lent a golden hue to her pale skin and set her auburn hair afire with bronze highlights.

A rapping on the door made her jump.

Ross opened it to a trio of servants bearing all the food and drink he had ordered. "Over there. On the sideboard, aye?

Quickly now. And light those candelabras as well. 'Tis much too dark in here." Hopefully, the additional light would be to her liking.

The servants hurried to fulfill his commands. Once finished, they scurried from the room.

"Do ye wish more to eat?" He peered under the cloth covering the platters, pleased at both the bounty and the quality.

"I think not," she said, her focus still fixed on the fire.

"Well, I desire a whisky and a seat by the hearth." He poured his drink, then glanced back at her. "Do ye wish one, m'lady? I'd like us to talk this time instead of sitting in silence as we did before." Earlier, she had remained mute, sipping her drink and staring into the flames. He would make no progress at winning her trust if that continued. Perhaps, if he employed the intimacy of using her name, she would open to him. "Wine or whisky, my dear Elise?"

Her head snapped up, and she turned with a jerk, staring at him with her lips parted. Color highlighted her cheeks, softening the hollows and adding to the emotions flashing in her eyes. "Wine, please," she finally uttered. Hands fisted at her sides, she lowered herself to perch on a chair in front of the hearth.

With wine in one hand and whisky in the other, he joined her by the fire and handed her the goblet before seating himself in the chair opposite her. "Now," he said, then took a sip while keeping his gaze locked with hers. "Tell me all about yerself."

Her mouth tightened. Leeriness shouted from her as she clasped her wine with both hands, as though fearing she might drop it. She lifted her chin but kept her face turned aside as if trying to keep her birthmark in the shadows. "Why?"

"Why?"

She made a nervous toss of her head, took a sip, then attempted a defiant, side-eyed glance. Her bravado failed. The fluttering tick of her pounding heart couldn't hide beneath the pale skin of her slender throat. The rapid rise and fall of her chest betrayed her as well. "What does it matter? My life? What difference does it make?"

"It matters because ye matter."

That made her scoot back in the seat, as if confused.

"I wish to know the woman who is now my wife. Is that so strange?" He rolled the glass between his hands, hoping he sounded surer of himself than he felt. "Do ye wish to know anything about me? I can go first if ye like."

"Please do," she said, sounding as though she needed time to rein in her panic.

He rose, always more comfortable on the move than seated. "I am the middle MacDougall son, descended from the line of Gareth. My father was constable to the fearsome *Gallóglaigh* warriors of Argyll as was his father before him, and his before him." He splashed a bit more whisky into his glass, then strolled back and forth across the length of the room. "My eldest brother, Thorburn, is constable now, but should he fall, the task comes to me. If I fail, it goes to my younger brother, Valan."

"That tells me nothing about yerself." She resettled in the chair as though wishing to be anywhere but where she was. "Tell me of Ross, the man. Not Commander Ross, the warrior."

That set him back and halted his pacing. Ross, the man. What could he tell her that she hadn't already heard? He loved women, whether they be maidservants, whores, or other men's wives. They usually loved him back, and that always caused a problem. So far as he knew, he had left behind no children with the frequent sowing of his seed, which made him wonder if something might be wrong with him. But he couldn't tell her that. What wife would wish to know such things about her husband?

"That's tied yer tongue, has it?" One of her feathery brows arched higher. "So, be it. Since ye've gone mute on anything other than warring, I have nothing to share that might interest ye, m'lord. I have never warred. I have only run from that which sought to destroy me."

So, she would challenge him. Good. That was a start. "Well played, dear wife."

He returned to his seat, determined to look her in the eyes as he spoke of something he rarely shared. "I will tell ye a thing I tell verra few." After a deep breath and a hearty exhale, he continued. "I watched my father die of a broken heart when we discovered my mother and little sister impaled on stakes and set ablaze." He paused and swallowed hard, nearly choking on the unbearable memory. "I swore to never give the entirety of my heart to anyone ever again. I couldna bear all that my father suffered, nor will I ever forget the pain of that carnage."

Her eyes flared wide, and all color left her face.

"Aye, it was a terrible time," he whispered. He bowed his head and closed his eyes, fighting to shove the horrific vision away as he had done so many times before. After a deep breath, he lifted his head. "But we survived it, my brothers and I. Lived to fight another day and avenge all the wrongs done to those we loved. With the ferocity and vengeance deserved." He hazarded a sip and then smoothed away the moisture on the rim of the glass with his thumb. "Now, m'lady, tell me of yer story."

Her gaze slid back to the fire as if the crackling flames strengthened her. As she brushed her fingertips across the red blotch staining her face, her mouth quivered with a weak smile. "Because of this..." Her fingers paused in the middle of the mark. "Mama protected me as much as she could." Her hand dropped to her lap. "Then she died while birthing my brother." After a deep breath, she gave a sad shake of her head. "And her death was all for naught because his tiny soul left for Heaven before hers." She emptied her glass and set it on the small table beside her chair. Hands clasped, she continued, "Father never could bear the sight of me." She twitched a defensive shrug. "He never harmed me, just behaved as though I never existed." The muscles in her thin face flexed. She worked her jaws as if the memories left a foul taste in her mouth. "Then he married again. A cruel, hateful woman." Her hands tightened into fists in her lap. "And she sold me to Lord Craevan, Earl of the Craevan Cliffs."

"Sold ye?" If she'd been sold into slavery, that explained her reaction every time he made any sudden movements around her.

She met his gaze. "Yes. Tricked the fool into paying for me instead of the other way around. Made up some ridiculous tale about my connection to a treasure my mother hid as a young woman." A bitter smile curled her lips. "A devious hag, my stepmother. Canny and ruthless. She wanted rid of me and filled her purse in the process."

"And yer father didna lift a finger to stop her?"

"Nay. He knew one as ugly as me would never marry and make a profitable alliance for him without a hefty dowry he wasna willing to pay." Her stark sadness somehow made her unrealized beauty even more stunning as she stared into the firelight. Her eyes closed, and she blew out a heavy sigh. "My father blamed me for my mother's death. Said the demon that marked me hungered for Mama, too." She bowed her head. "And such is my lot in life now because of my curse." She opened her eyes and glared at him. "I am thankful for my flawed appearance. It has protected me well." She stared at him as though suddenly realizing he sat right in front of her. "At least until now." Sitting taller, she jutted her chin to a defiant angle and looked him in the eyes. "With any hope, my face will revolt ye just as it has others." A resentful smile frosted the iciness in her eyes even more. "I remained a virgin wife once. 'Tis my hope to do so again."

"Virgin wife?" Craevan hadn't bought her to be a slave or a servant, but a wife? But if that were so…

She wrinkled her nose as though she wished she could snatch the words back. With a flick of her hand, she blew out a disgusted snort. "I should not have said that."

"Obviously not." Ross rose for another whisky. "I assume the Earl of Craevan is still yer husband?"

"Yes." She stood and faced him. "And I *assume* ye wish to take back that ye never beat women?"

He refused to grace that with an answer. "The man still lives?" If he did, then Ross didn't have a wife. Wouldn't that give the Lord of Argyll a burning case of the red arse? A chuckle escaped him before he could stop it.

She stared at him, her defiant scowl turning to one of confusion. "Yes, he lives, and as ye've realized, that makes our union void."

"Aye, that be true." His smile faded, and he scrubbed a hand across his jaw. "But if the MacDougall gets wind of it, there'll be hell to pay." He locked eyes with her, willing her to see the severity of the situation. "And he'll not take it out on me, lass."

"If he sends me back to Ireland, the Earl of Connacht will order me beaten to death."

"What about yer husband?" He found it strange she didn't seem all that concerned about Craevan.

With a snort and another flip of her hand, she returned to her seat in front of the fire. "I doubt he even knows I'm gone." A bitter laugh escaped her. "He gobbled down that ridiculous tale of treasure as if it were cake." She cocked her head and gave him the loveliest smile she had managed since he met her. "He has other women. He only married me to fulfill some ridiculous prophecy my stepmother made him believe. Arnella is quite the storyteller."

"But if he married ye to gain treasure, do ye not think he'll attempt to recover ye for it?" A greedy man wouldn't cast aside the opportunity of easy wealth. She needed to realize that.

With a half-hearted smile, she reached to unwind the elaborate braid coiled around her head. Once her freed tresses flowed down her back, she ran her hand along her nape, then pulled forward a hank of hair shorter than all the rest. "While I never heard my stepmother's lie in full, one requirement other than marrying me must have been to cut off some of my hair for some sort of ritual." She released it and tossed her head, combing her fingers back through her thick wavy hair and unfurling the braid. "He cut it on our wedding night and never touched me again. A fortnight later, he took three of the servants indebted to him the most and left on some sort of crusade." She shrugged. "I assume it was to seek the treasure since he sold every stick of furniture in his keep to pay for supplies for the trip."

"And that is when ye made yer escape?"

"Yes." She rubbed her arms as though chilled and returned to the fire. "Foolishly, I attempted to run the day after our wedding. His priest caught me and brought me back." Her expression turned thoughtful. "Craevan had already cut my hair but still refused to release me. Said he needed a servant since he was down to so few, and the woman who usually cooked for him had died." She picked up the blackened iron leaning against the hearth and poked the fire until the logs roared with stronger flames. "But once he left, I waited for the priest to drink himself into his usual stupor and got away." She frowned as she leaned the rod back against the hearth. "And then Connacht's men captured me when I took the wrong path and wandered too close to their squabble with another clan. That's when I decided my curse had gained strength." She retrieved her glass and held it out. "Might I have another, m'lord?

"Of course." He took the glass, then paused. "Call me Ross, aye?" The more he learned about her, the more he wished to know about this woman who had no idea of either her worth or her beauty. All she knew was the battle to survive. "After all, we are married."

"No," she reminded gently. "We are not. As I told ye, Craevan lives."

He filled her glass, a wily plot coming together as the ruby red liquid gurgled into the cup. With his whisky refreshed as well, he returned to her and offered the drink. "I have a proposition for ye."

She eyed him, took the drink, and downed a healthy swallow. "I am listening."

"Ye know ye would be safer as my wife—or at least appearing to be my wife." He swirled the whisky in the cup. The golden liquid's reflection helped him think and choose the proper words. "With winter nearly upon us, ye need a safe haven, ye ken? Once spring comes and the weather's not as fierce, I'll take ye wherever ye wish to start a new life and see ye settled proper."

"And I would be free to live as I wished?" She didn't believe him. He could see it in her eyes.

"Aye, Elise. Ye'd be free as the wind. I've helped other victims relocate. I can do the same for yerself." He grinned and lifted his glass in a toast. "I'm nay just a handsome warrior, ye ken? There are times when a sword doesna solve every problem."

"Ye lie." She ignored his lifted glass and refused to touch hers to it. "What true *Gallóglaigh* warrior speaks such nonsense?"

"Do ye have a better place to spend the winter than at my side?" That gave her pause. He forced himself not to smile, even though he loved gloating when he was right.

"What do ye require of me in exchange?" She emptied her glass and squared her shoulders as if bracing herself for the worst.

"Yer trust," he said, then quietly added, "And yer friendship."

Her gaze slid to the floor, and a sad smile pulled a corner of her mouth higher than the other. "Trust and friendship, ye say?"

Her suddenly muted spirit, almost like disappointment, confused him. "Aye, Elise, nothing more than trust and friendship. I swear." What had he said to make her sad of a sudden? The hour grew late. Perhaps she feared he intended to demand her maidenhead as down payment. "And dinna fash yerself, lass. I shall make a pallet for myself on the floor in front of the hearth." He gave her his biggest smile. "The bed is all yers, my fine lady."

She turned and eyed the massive, canopied bed, its curtains already closed except for the foot and the side closest to the fire. "Perhaps we should retire then." A shudder shook across her delicate frame, then she squared her shoulders. "If weather permits, we leave tomorrow, yes?"

"Aye." He tossed back his drink and placed the glass on the table beside hers. "We'll need to be well rested not only for the journey but for whatever we find once we arrive at our new homestead." The day had taken a toll on him as well. So much so that he might not even bother with a pallet. He'd slept propped in a chair before.

With a toss of her chin in his direction, she spun a finger in midair. "Turn then, so I might ready myself for the bed."

"Do ye need help with yer laces?" Ross wasn't a stranger to the challenges of stripping a lady down to her shift. At her lifted brow, he held up both hands and added, "I willna look. I'll just loosen yer laces and then turn away, so ye may do whatever ye must."

Again, her countenance fell and something akin to sadness bowed her head.

What had he said this time? "I wasna trying to offend ye, Elise."

With another half-smile, she shrugged. "I know." She came closer and held out her arms. "Sleeves first please and then the side ties, if ye would. Florie took them in as tight as she could since the lady who once wore this dress was a mite bigger than me."

Everyone was bigger than Elise, but he bit his tongue to keep from saying it. With a deftness from years of experience, he loosened her sleeves, then undid the ties laced at her sides. Her pale skin flushed with color that crept across her décolletage, then climbed her throat and deepened the redness of her cheeks until her faint dusting of freckles disappeared.

His trews became entirely too tight, and he prayed his surcoat would hide the bulge of his rising. She would never trust him if she spied his cock hard as the iron rod beside the hearth.

He stepped back and gave her his back, folding his hands in front of his manparts to keep them properly concealed. "I shall stay like this until ye tell me ye're covered. Never fear—contrary to what some may say, I can behave myself when I so choose."

"Thank ye, Commander Ross," came her quiet reply, her melancholy tone still puzzling.

"Call me *Ross*, aye?"

"Yes." A rustling of material, then the sound of hurried footsteps followed. The lights flickered out, cloaking the room in shadows. Apparently, she had doused most of the candles. "Sleep well, Ross," she said from the direction of the bed.

He turned and found her covered to her chin, her gaze fixed on him. Her lush, wavy hair splayed across the pillows made him swallow hard. He'd always had a weakness for fiery-haired lasses. Aye, 'twas best he sleep by the fire and not go anywhere near that bed.

"Sleep well, Elise." He settled into a chair and crossed his legs at the ankles, hoping his cock would soon sleep, too.

CHAPTER FOUR

"I HATE YE," Elise whispered, knotting her fist in the corner of her pillow.

Ross's relaxed form silhouetted by the firelight infuriated her. Made her feel uglier than she ever had before. She poured all her wretchedness into a hard glare, daring him to look toward the bed. Notice her. Rise from that blasted chair and climb under the covers with her. Make her know what it was like to be needed. Wanted. More than anything, she wanted to be wanted. Just once. Her eyes burned with the need to weep for all the years of loneliness, but she couldn't give in and cry. If she did, she might never stop.

Besides, fools hoping for impossible things didn't deserve the right to weep. And that's what she was. A dunderheaded fool. Why in Heaven's name would a man like Commander Ross wish to seduce her? She rolled to her back and stared up at the canopy, berating herself for such idiotic weakness. A wise woman would be thankful to be left alone. Once again, her face had protected her maidenhead.

Not that she wished to be ravished. But what woman didn't dream of being held with some small amount of tenderness? And kissed. She had never received a proper kiss. Well, at least not one with any ardor. She threw off the bedcovers, kicking them to the foot of the bed. Shame on her for wanting any of that. Since when did she even think of such things?

Since Ross. It was his fault. The man was too kind. Respectful. Protective to a fault. She flopped to her other side and focused on the folds of the velvety bed curtain. Even when she baited him, he responded with nothing but kindness.

"He regrets calling ye a boy child," she hissed into the darkness. When he stood there in front of the Lord of Toads and bowed his head in shame, her jaw almost dropped in surprise. 'Twas the guilt that made him wed her with no argument, and she'd not missed his relief when she told him about being married to Craevan and that the oaf still lived. He even laughed out loud. His joy at his newfound freedom hurt as much as a beating.

She sat up, pummeled her pillow, and threw herself back down to stare at his reclining shadow some more. What a fool she was. She squeezed her eyes shut, determined to sleep and escape this lonely hell if only for a brief few hours until morning. But she couldn't. The sound of his breathing filled the room. And his snoring. Holy hell, the man sounded like an overfed dog stretched out in front of the hearth. That hurt her feelings even more. Had he fallen asleep as soon as his arse hit the chair? Even though he knew her to be in the bed wearing nothing but a shift? Was she that easy to cast from his mind?

"I hate ye," she whispered again.

"That's twice ye've said that now. Why do ye hate me, lass?"

She bit her lip and held her breath. He had snored as if deep in slumber. Surely, he'd spoken in his sleep.

He shifted, scooted higher in the chair, and recrossed his legs at the ankles. "Elise—why do ye hate me? I have tried to show ye nothing but kindness and respect. I even apologized for the cruelty in the great hall. Tell me, lass. How have I failed ye? What more can I do?"

"Ye were snoring." She yanked the covers back up over herself as a shield from his questions.

"Ye hate me because I snore?"

"No. Ye were asleep. Yer loud snorting echoed through the

room."

"I snort because my nose is broken. I was trying in vain to pull some air through it. Forgive me for disturbing ye." He turned her way, but she couldn't see his face because of the fire behind him. "If ye dinna hate me because of my snoring, then why Elise? Tell me true. Remember I said ye can always speak yer mind to me. I willna harm ye."

"I hate ye because ye make me know..." She couldn't confess it all, because then he would agree with her, and it would be too painful to bear. Life had always been surviving one cruelty after another. But of late, her strength, her resolve, her self-worth had taken such a massive beating, she didn't know how much more she could endure.

"I make ye know what?" He pushed himself to his feet and eased toward her, smooth and silent as a beast stalking its prey. Apparently, he'd kicked off his boots while she wrestled with her demons. "Tell me, lass. I make ye know what?"

"Ye make me know how ugly I am." There. She said it. She clenched her teeth, waiting for his response that would surely make her misery worse.

He halted, his expression still unreadable because of the shadows. She wished she hadn't blown out all the candles on her side of the room. The only ones still burning were those on the mantel behind him.

"I have never said you were anything but lovely." He bowed his head. At least she could make that out in the darkness. "Again, I beg yer forgiveness for thinking ye a wee laddie. But it was because of the filth and the clothes—not because of yerself." Without warning, he closed the distance between them and sat on the edge of the bed beside her. "Ye're nay ugly or repulsive, and I'll thrash anyone who says ye are."

"I dinna want ye to thrash anyone," she said softly. "I just want ye to want me."

"Ye what?"

"I willna say it again. 'Twas hard enough to say the first

time." She clutched the covers up to her chin, wishing she'd held her tongue, so he would go away. "Forgive me for keeping ye from yer sleep." With a shooing motion toward the chair, she scooted deeper into her pillows. "Go back to yer seat. I'll trouble ye no more with my silliness."

"Nay, lass," he said as he stripped off his shirt and let it fall to the floor. "I willna sleep in the chair tonight."

Something akin to fear but a great deal hotter and more breathtaking in an exciting sort of way shot through her. "Where will ye sleep then?"

"With my wife." He lifted the covers and slid into the bed.

She scooted away so quickly that she nearly fell off the other side. "Ye dinna have a wife, remember? Our marriage isna real. Ye said so yerself. Laughed about it even. Thrilled and relieved ye were about discovering yer freedom."

He reached out and trailed a finger along her cheek. "And in so doing, I hurt ye again. Did I not?"

Unable to speak, she managed a quick nod but prayed he wouldn't draw away.

"I didna laugh because our marriage contract was void." He eased closer, the heat of him wrapping her in an embrace the likes of which she had never hoped for. "I laughed because the MacDougall didna realize he'd been outwitted by the fine woman he treated so coarsely."

That deep rumbling of his voice. The soft touch of his breath against her skin. Everything about him mesmerized her. Made it impossible to think or speak, much less breathe. Her heartbeat pounded in her ears. Surely, this had to be a dream. She would open her eyes and find him back in that infernal chair.

"I do want ye, Elise. I wanted ye earlier when I helped ye with yer laces." He brushed her hair away from her face and cradled her cheek in his palm. "But I didna wish to frighten ye or make ye think ye had to submit simply because ye're trapped here with me."

A terrible thought broke through her delicious daze, making

her hitch in a sharp gasp. "Ye dinna think me a whore, do ye?"

He slid closer, curled an arm beneath her, and pulled her closer. "I think ye beautiful, fearless, and determined. Only good things come to mind when I think of ye, m'lady." His thumb traced the line of her bottom lip as though memorizing its shape. "But are ye certain, Elise? Do ye truly wish to become one, even though I'm nay yer legal husband?"

She couldn't speak and tell him all that stormed within her. The aching loneliness. The burning need to know something other than scorn or hatred. Yes, she would gladly become one with this man even if it was only for a night. She found the courage to press her hand to the center of his hard, muscular chest. His heartbeat tickled against her palm, making her smile. "I do," she whispered.

His kisses started slow and gentle, then increased in intensity like a storm building at sea. She smoothed her hand across the ridges of his chest, marveling how his skin could feel like velvet yet the strength beneath it rippled hard as stone. He rolled her to her back while nuzzling underneath her jawline and down her throat. With an abrupt pause, he unfastened his trews, slid them off, then kicked them to the floor. Then he lay back beside her and pulled her close, teasing her with flitting touches that made her arch against him.

He slid his hand down her arm, took her hand, and placed it on his long, rigid cock.

She wrapped her fingers around its thickness. Sudden panic at its size made her cough as though about to choke. That thing would split her in two. How in the world could she bear it?

"Dinna worry, m'love," he whispered as he kissed her chemise off her shoulders. "We willna rush anything. Ye're nay ready just yet." He pushed her shift aside and slid his hand inside. His nibbling along her collarbone made her forget her worries and arch to curl a leg around his hip.

He kissed his way lower, forcing the gown down past her waist, then slipped it off completely. The cool air across her nakedness fanned the flames of her yearning, making her press closer. She needed the feel of his flesh sliding against hers. Her nipples still tingled because of his tongue, making her slow to realize he was licking his way lower. As he passed her navel, she laced her fingers in his hair. He knew so many wondrous ways to make her shiver. She daren't imagine what might come next.

A squeak escaped her as he pressed his face between her legs and dipped his tongue inside. She never knew such pleasure existed. His fingertips tickled up her inner thighs. Teasing. Taunting. Making her groan and pull him harder against her. As he served her, he slipped one finger and then two deep inside her slippery wetness. She couldn't bear it anymore. Wave after wave of bliss shot through her, making her cry out. Gasping for air, unsure whether to weep, laugh, or scream, she shuddered and bucked beneath his touch.

He nuzzled a trail of kisses from her mouth to the tender skin behind her ear. "Do ye trust me, love?"

Still catching her breath, she managed a nod. Yes. She trusted him. All that he'd just made her feel was indescribable. "I trust ye. Do what ye will. But be quick about it, aye?" The heat of him against her front paired with his squeezing of her backside made her yearn for more of those blissful waves crashing through her core.

Slipping his knee between hers, he gently parted her legs and settled down between them. "Try to relax, love," he murmured against her mouth.

Relax? Surely, he jested. Every fiber of her being felt taut and ready to snap. "I'll try," she lied, arching up to nudge against the hard length of him.

He pushed inside a short way, then stopped and held fast, trembling.

Was that it? She wrapped her legs around him and squeezed. The fullness was nice, but surely that wasn't all?

"Ye're tight as the hole in a new barrel," he groaned, with his forehead against her shoulder as he inched in a little farther.

"Is that good or bad?" She didn't wish to disappoint. After all, her part had been quite nice so far.

"'Tis wondrous as long as I dinna hurt ye." He pushed deeper, but still held himself slightly above her.

She slid a hand to the back of his head, held tight, and whispered against his ear, "More—please."

"Gladly, m'lady." A hard shove buried him to the hilt and nested him well between her thighs. Then he slid out and drove in deep again. And again. Each time a little faster.

As he pounded, she clutched at his sides, arching upward to meet him thrust for thrust. The blessed waves returned with a vengeance, making her keen out the pleasure too great to contain.

Her shriek made him pound harder until he roared like a caged beast, then locked in place and shook with repeated spasms.

He propped on his elbows to keep from crushing her as he went still and sagged atop her. "M'lady," he groaned, pressing his forehead to hers, then brushing her mouth with a tender kiss.

"M'lord." She hugged him close, delighting in the weight of him. "Was it all right?" she whispered into the darkness. After all that he had done for her, she didn't wish to leave him wanting.

"More than just all right, Elise." He rolled to his side but kept her in his arms. With her face framed in one hand, he held her so she couldn't look away. "Are ye all right, m'lady? Shall I fetch ye some water and a cloth?"

A sudden shyness overcame her. "Uhm... I can manage, thank ye." She made to slide out of the bed, but he halted her.

"Stay here where it's warm, love. I shall fetch it."

Unashamed of his grand nakedness, he rose and strode to the corner of the room where the washstand and chamberpot chair stood. The sight of him made her smile. How could such a man treat her so well? She had never thought herself worthy of such after so many cruel remarks and beatings. But now, this man, this dear sweet soul, swore he thought only good things about her.

He returned with a damp cloth in one hand, a bottle under his arm, and a pair of glasses in the other. He smiled as he held out the rag. "Ye may be a bit sore tomorrow, but the water should help with that. Florie left herbs floating in it. I believe she will be a fine lady's maid for ye after all."

"Florie is verra kind." She took the cloth, then stared up at him, too embarrassed to clean herself up while he watched.

He started as though someone had poked him. "Forgive me." With a quick turn, he gave her the privacy of his back while he filled the glasses. "I thought a toast would be in order."

She had to admit, whatever Florie put in the water left her lady parts tingling. The blood on the bedsheets gave her pause, then she smiled. She had rid herself of that cursed maidenhead at last. Perhaps now her fate would improve. "What are we toasting?" she asked as she lobbed the cloth across the room and hit the bowl with a splash and a plop.

"Well done, lass." Ross handed her the glass and then held his aloft. "To trust," he said with a look that made her shiver.

A shiver not from cold, but renewed warmth. She wondered if he felt that same simmering heat. A glance downward confirmed he did. His wondrous manhood stood erect and ready.

She lifted her glass and touched it to his. "To trust and a prosperous union." Perhaps she shouldn't have added that. Especially when she'd as much as promised that as soon as spring came, she would no longer be his problem. But she couldn't help it. The words came out before she could call them back.

His smile grew even brighter. "Aye, m'love. To trust and a prosperous union indeed."

They both downed their drinks. He refilled them both before settling with his back against the headboard. "I must say 'tis nice to relax in the bed with a lovely woman."

A twinge of jealousy flitted through her, but she brushed it aside. The past couldn't be changed. "Did ye ever intend to marry?" Most men did, if only to secure a woman to do their sewing, cooking, and cleaning. They could get carnal pleasures anywhere. Someone to manage the other chores? Not so easy to find without an abundance of coin.

He frowned and tilted his head to the side as though deep in thought. After a slow sip of his drink, he shook his head. "Nay. I hardened my heart against love and marriage when I saw how that tenderness weakened my father, and in the end, killed him. If he'd nay loved my mother and sister so verra much, I know he'd be alive to this day."

"So, ye will never love? Or marry?" That made her sad. She didn't hope for more than she had already received. In fact, she knew better than to even dream of anything more. But Ross deserved better. Such a kind generous man deserved the pleasure of a happy home, filled with the laughter of his bairns. "Will ye not be lonely in yer old age?"

"I live for now," he replied quietly. With a gentle pull, he slid her over to sit beside him. "Today is the only thing guaranteed because it is the present. Tomorrow may never come. Nor the day after." He kissed her long and slow. She savored the taste of the whisky on his lips.

"In that case, I think we should have another glass, then ye can continue my lessons." She held out her empty glass, her middle warm from the fiery brew and the man beside her.

"Yer lessons?" He quirked a brow as he tipped the bottle and poured more of the golden nectar into her cup.

She smiled and lightly clinked her glass to his. "I believe the herbs Florie added to the water did a mite more than ease any soreness." With a brazenness she'd never seen in herself before, she took hold of his member and squeezed with a firm up and down pull. "It's filled me with a tingle that I fear only ye can sate."

"Has it now?" He downed his drink, set the glass aside, and groaned as she pulled harder. He placed his hand on top of hers. "Like this, love. But place yerself across my legs so I can stoke yer fires, too."

As soon as she repositioned, he tantalized her with those

masterful fingers, making her pump him harder. "Oh my," she said, "It takes concentration to enjoy what ye're doing and ensure what I'm doing pleases ye, too."

"Aye, love. That it does." He placed his thumb against a tender spot and added to his artful caressing. "How about this? Does that pleasure ye?"

Pleasure her? It drove her mad. Not to be outdone and hoping that what she intended was not wrong, she took him in her mouth as far as it would go.

"God's beard!" He bucked upward and knotted a fist in the sheet as he massaged her faster, as though their pleasuring had become a race.

She would ask if this was right, but at the moment, it wasn't possible to speak. So, she sucked harder, hoping he would advise her if this was wrong.

"I canna take anymore!" He grabbed her up, spread her across the bed, and drove into her. "Mercy, woman," he groaned. "I must have ye."

She welcomed him back, proud she had brought him to such a state. But her pride soon disappeared, replaced by the return of the thundering sensations Ross unleashed with masterful stroking. She pressed upward, meeting each of his thrusts and crying out when the indescribable ecstasy overpowered her.

He growled and pounded harder, then settled deep and spasmed, emptying inside her.

In secret, a small part of her prayed. Prayed that a babe might take root and grow. A child to love who would love her back. A silly notion since she planned to leave and start a new life come spring. But she would make this wish and keep it locked away as long as this kind generous man chose to spill his seed within her. She held him tight, reveling in all that was him, and the warm delicious bond, the likes of which she had never known.

THE ANGRY HOWL of the storm and the sleet and rain lashing against the window mesmerized him. It would be dawn soon, and he had yet to sleep a wink. No matter. Ross trained himself long ago to go days on with nothing more than a few minutes of stolen rest here and there. Elise slept in the crook of his arm, curled against him like a wee kitten with her head nestled in the dip of his shoulder. His wife. He swallowed hard against the sudden burn of bile at the back of his throat. What the hell was he to do with a wife?

He had never felt so much guilt and responsibility about taking a maidenhead in all his life. They might not be wed according to the church, Scotland, or England, but in the eyes of God Almighty, they were one. He heard the edict in his head. In his mother's voice, in fact. So loud and clear, his cock shrank and tried to hide between his bollocks and his thigh. Elise O'Cleirigh was Elise O'Cleirigh MacDougall, no matter if her first legal husband still walked the earth or not. That man hadn't claimed her virginity, Ross had.

But perhaps what disturbed him most was the growing fondness he felt stirring in his chest. And the need to protect her against everyone and everything that had ever hurt her or might attempt to hurt her again. He'd never experienced such a dangerous ailment with any woman before. But Elise differed from his other conquests. As petite and delicate as a spirit of the glen, she possessed the passion and fury of a mighty fae queen— even after so many had attacked that fury with their cruelties.

She stirred against him, nuzzling closer. A peaceful sigh escaped her as she tucked her arm tighter to her chest.

She must be chilled. He worked the bedclothes higher and tucked them up over her shoulders, then curled his arm back around her. Would marriage be such a bad thing? The wind howled louder as if shouting an answer. Whether the storm said yay or nay, he couldn't tell. Thorburn seemed contented enough with Adellis and their wee son, Mathan. But—

"What ails ye?" Elise whispered through a hitching yawn.

"Ye're twitching like a cat about to pounce."

"Forgive me, love." He hugged her closer. "Just listening to the storm. Go back to sleep, aye? I'll try to stop my twitching." He kissed the top of her head and rested his cheek against it.

"Might we have to stay here longer? Because of the storm?"

As much as he wanted to say *no*, there was no denying that could happen. "We'll not know 'til morning."

"It is morning. Well past sunrise even." She pushed herself upright and smiled down at him as though she thought him a silly child. "Look at the night candle. Not even a stub left. Just melted wax all over the dresser. That'll be a bugger to clean."

"A *bugger*, eh?" He chuckled at the mild profanity.

She covered her mouth as though ashamed, but even in the dim light, he caught the mischievous sparkle in her eyes.

"Sorry. I shouldna speak that way." She hitched over to the edge of the bed, snatched up one of the extra blankets, and wrapped it around herself as she stood.

"Come back to bed." He didn't care if it was morning. As long as they stayed in the bed, they could ignore the real world and all its complications.

"I have things demanding my attention." As she lifted the side of the heavy tapestry covering the window, she tossed him a pointed look. "A gentleman would face the other direction, so I might have a bit of privacy with the chamberpot."

"Whatever ye command, my lady." He rolled to his side, smiling at the ease of their conversation this morning. Yesterday, whenever they spoke, the words had come out stilted. Forced. Almost like a pair of warriors circling one another, waiting to see who would attack first. Today, he sensed some trust, and it pleased him.

"'Tis a dreich day outside. Least I think that's what ye Scot's call it." The grayness of the room became a shade darker as she let the tapestry fall back in place.

"And what do the Irish call it?"

"Tuesday."

Laughter rumbled from him, and he almost forgot and rolled over to face her.

"Daren't ye do it!" she scolded. "I've barely begun my morning ablutions."

"Ye are my wife, ye ken?"

"Pretend wife," she corrected, her somber tone making him wish he hadn't broached the subject.

And that's when he decided. Mother would be proud, and he could almost see her smiling down from Heaven above. He didn't roll over, but he spoke louder to ensure Elise didn't miss a word. "Nay, my love. Ye are my wife. In the eyes of God Almighty. Ye gifted me yer maidenhead and when I took it, ye became mine for all time."

No response. The silence of the room broken only by the sound of splashing water.

"Elise?"

"I heard ye," she said quietly.

At the pinging sound of the fire iron hitting the hearthstones, he pushed himself upward and sat on the side of the bed.

With the blanket still wrapped around her, Elise stirred the banked coals, then added several sticks of wood. She stared down at them, the iron still in her hand.

He rose and joined her at the hearth, seating himself in one of the chairs. "We can have yer first marriage annulled, then ours will be legal. Or if ye wish, we can do ours all over again after the annulment."

She shifted her frown from the fire to him. "Why?"

"So ye can be my wife, and I can protect ye."

Her lips pressed into a flat line, trembling as she fought for control. "I dinna want yer pity or yer charity."

"Good. Because I'll nay be giving ye either." He clenched his teeth and pulled in a deep breath, reminding himself that it would take more than one night of loving to exorcise all the ghosts of her past. "And while we're about it, I'm nay expecting any fawning gratitude from yerself." He rose and closed the distance between them, took the iron rod out of her hand, and leaned it against the hearth. As she stepped away, he caught hold of her shoulders and forced her to stand fast. "We have this winter to live as man and wife. If at the end of that time, ye still wish to leave and make a new life alone, I shall keep my word and help ye do so. But if ye decide being my wife isna such a terrible fate after all, then we shall keep it so. Agreed?" A determination to make her see the sense of staying with him, allowing him to protect her well past spring, settled within him. And when he decided something, he made it so. "Agreed?" he repeated.

Her gaze held fast with his. She jerked with a defiant lift of her chin. "Agreed."

"Good." He swept her up into his arms and turned toward the bed.

"And just what do ye think ye're doing?"

"I am going to make love to my wife," he said. "'Tis the finest way I know to start the day."

CHAPTER FIVE

"**G**OD HELP US make it." After a silent *amen,* Elise crossed herself, then tightened her grip on the throat of her fur-lined hood to keep the wind from yanking it off her head. 'Twas far less than a fine day to move to a new home but, given the choice of the storm or another day at Dunstaffnage, she still chose the storm.

Sandwiched between Munro, Ross's provisions knave, and Florie on the seat of the wagon, she squinted to see through the bone-chilling mix of rain, sleet, and snow. After struggling to find Ross, she spotted him sitting tall and proud on his monstrous hairy-footed steed. The knot in her chest eased. With his furry cloak draped across his shoulders, he looked like a great, shaggy beast. Thank goodness he appeared strong and hearty against the fierce weather.

"Are ye all right, m'lady?" Florie shouted over the roar of the wind. She reached over and tugged Elise's cloak closer around her and adjusted the fur across her lap. "Need ye another fur? Or a pair of dry mittens?"

"Dinna be fussing after me, silly girl." Elise softened the scolding with a smile. "Just tuck in and share the pelt, so we'll both be warmer."

Florie smiled and scooted closer. She leaned across and tugged on Munro's sleeve. "How much farther?"

The man scowled at her, his bushy black brows and beard

frosted with freezing droplets. "I believe we might be two wagon lengths closer than the last time ye asked." He flipped the reins to encourage the team to keep plodding onward through the freezing mud. "We'll get there when we get there, ye ken?"

"Cross bugger," Florie said, countering his scowl with a fierce look of her own.

Elise smiled and snuggled deeper into her cloak. The two had been fussing since the onset of the trip.

Ross came up beside them, squinting as the deluge pelted him in the face. "How fare ye, m'lady?"

Soaked to the skin, half-frozen, and the bones of her arse ready to split through her flesh if she bounced on this hard bench one more time. But rather than whine like a spoiled bairn, she forced a bright smile. "I am well. Just ready to be there."

He gave her a nod, then veered his mount to the other wagons behind them. Eight in total. Three with enough supplies to get them through the winter. Three with building materials, cookware, and furniture. And the last two with cages of chickens, geese, ducks, and young pigs.

Ross's brother Valan and his two knaves brought up the rear with four fine Highland cows and a combined herd of goats and sheep.

The wagons and livestock seemed a bit much since they didn't even know if a roof remained to shelter themselves, much less protect the animals. And what about feed? Animals needed to eat just like they did. When Ross told her not to worry, she held her tongue. He didn't understand. She'd lived a cursed life long enough to warrant worry. But no. She wouldn't act the ungrateful wretch. Besides, her situation had vastly improved. Whatever came, she would handle it by counting her blessings rather than caterwauling about all that had gone wrong before.

The wagon lurched and bounced. She flinched as her arse hit the bench as hard as a smithy's hammer coming down on an anvil.

"When we get there, I'll fix ye a good soak of herbs. I'm sure ye're...tender." Florie gave a knowing look from the depths of her hood.

"I'll be happy with a fire and a place in the dry." All she heard about Tòrrelise had not sounded promising. She imagined a pile of tumbled-down rocks and nothing more. Hopefully, the mound of stone would at least be large enough to shield them all from the wind.

Someone shouted, but she couldn't make out what they said. Munro pulled on the reins, and the wagon lurched to a stop.

"What is it?" She tried to read his expression, but he looked as ill-tempered as he had when they set out. "Munro! What is it?"

After a snorting huff that fogged in the frigid air, Munro gave her a sideways glare. "We have arrived, m'lady. Welcome to yer new home."

She rolled her eyes at the man's attitude. With a nudge against Florie, she waved her onward. "Come. Master Munro says we have arrived. Let us see what we face."

Before they floundered free of the blankets and furs and climbed down, Ross rode up. He dismounted and offered to help them, but not before shooting a hard scowl at the man still seated on the bench. "Munro! I will speak with ye about yer lack of manners once the ladies are out of earshot, ye ken? There are plenty who would welcome the job of a provisions knave. Dinna think I will hesitate to replace ye."

Munro's sour expression melted, and his entire body slumped with an apologetic bowing of his head. "Forgive me, m'lord. I didna mean to be such an arse." With one eye squinted shut, he glared at the low-hanging clouds. "'Tis so feckin' cold and miserable."

"He's mad 'cause I dragged him outta Molly's bed," shouted another man who Ross had introduced as Tam, his weaponry knave. The grinning lad took charge of Ross's horse and led it away. "I shall see what shape the stable's in, m'lord," he said to Ross, then shot another taunting leer in Munro's direction. "Get yer lazy arse movin', Munro. There's work to be done, ye old bastard."

"Arse wipe," Munro countered as he leapt down from the wagon and trudged off.

Ross helped Florie down, then held up his hands to Elise. "Come, m'lady. Our home awaits." As soon as her feet touched the ground, he curled an arm around her and shielded her as much as he could from the wind. His attentiveness warmed her heart. Since she was already half-frozen and soaked to the bone, there was little he could do, but at least he made the effort.

"And there it is," he announced as he halted. "May God Almighty help us get through the winter."

She lifted her sagging hood and peered out. A sense of relief flooded her. The tight knot in her chest, the dread that made breathing so hard, cut loose and allowed her to pull in a deep breath of the chilly air. "Why, this is not so bad at all." She rushed forward, squinting through the angry weather. "I stayed in worse than this while on the run in Ireland."

"Aye, but that was summer."

"Maybe so, but summers in Ireland can be wet and cold when they've a mind to." A shiver made her pull her furry cloak closer. "Granted, not as cold as this, but still cold enough." She pointed at the crumbling broch. The tower loomed much taller than she had expected, making up one corner of the battered curtain wall guarding the buildings inside. "It's not fallen all that much. To be sure, we'll need to take care and check all the floors to make sure they're solid, but the part that's still standing looks hardy enough." Ignoring the water streaming down her face, she slogged into the center courtyard. She pointed at a row of small cottages connected to each other by a shared wall between them. "I'm sure their thatching needs some repair but look through their doorways. Most seem dry inside." Glancing back at Ross, she motioned toward the nearest open doorway. "Where are the doors and shutters?"

As he joined her, he slowly shook his head. "Who's to say? 'Tis my hope they're lying about somewhere. If not, we'll have to build more."

"First, we must get the animals inside the wall and find them shelter."

"Animals before people?" He stared at her with a perplexed knotting of his brows.

"Animals canna be expected to take care of us if we dinna have the good sense to take care of them." A long building to the right of the tower, the rear of it connected to the skirting wall, looked large enough to house all the livestock, including the horses that pulled the wagons and the men's mounts. She gave a determined nod at the structure. "Right there shall be our stable."

"That's a barracks for men." Ross turned her toward a much smaller structure to the left of a gaping hole in the barricade wall. "I believe that's the stable."

"Since we are not raising an army, we don't need a barracks." At his arched brow, she spoke louder to drown out both the storm and any argument he might give. "All of us shall do nicely enough inside the broch. That wing to the left of it looks to be attached. Probably the kitchen. There's sure to be extra room in there so everyone is sheltered."

He swiped the weather from his face, only to become drenched again as he studied her through the rain. "Is that how ye wish it?"

"That is how I wish it." It felt strange to say those words. No one since Mama had cared about what she wished. Of course, no one ever said they would be her husband just so they could protect her, either. She still didn't know what to think of that. Well, it wasn't that she didn't know—it was that she feared to think about it overlong because when she did, her heart hurt in a strange kind of way. Not an unpleasant hurt but a dangerous one. If she allowed a fondness for Ross to grow, the fates would steal him from her. And besides, she still planned on leaving come spring. Although the desire to carry that plan through dimmed with each passing day in Ross's presence. She jolted herself free of the treacherous musings. "Florie and I shall get to work in the tower, whilst ye get the animals settled." She started to rush away, then stopped and turned back. "That is all right? What I said we would do? Ye're certain of it?"

With a lopsided smile, he closed the distance between them and kissed the tip of her nose. "Absolutely, my wife. If ye're happy, I am happy."

For the first time since the journey started, her cheeks burned with heat. She ducked deeper into her hood and spun away. "Good then," she called back, then headed toward Florie, who was busy picking up broken bits of wood and toting them in her apron. When she reached the maid, she pointed at the broch. "Perhaps there'll be dry wood inside to start a fire. Come."

Florie nodded but kept hold of the wet fuel as they slogged through the mud. When they reached the door, Elise grabbed hold of the rusty iron ring with both hands and pulled. The heavy oak door, in the shape of a cathedral's arch and twice as tall as Ross, didn't budge. Reinforced with strips of iron and massive bolts and hinges, it just sat there and stared at her.

"Reckon it's locked?" Florie asked, blinking away the rain hitting her in the face.

Elise looked the door up and down. "There's no place for a key." She eyed the hinges, running her fingers along the cold metal. "We should push instead of pull. Old as this place is, I'd wager there's a bar to place across the inside of the door when they wish to keep everyone out."

"Together then, aye?" Florie placed her shoulder against the door. "Ready when ye are, m'lady."

With the hardest lunge she had in her, Elise hit the door. It flew open so fast they tumbled inside, landing in a pile on the floor. Florie exploded with hearty laughter, her joyous peals echoing through the chamber. Elise couldn't help herself. She joined in, christening her new home with mirth.

They helped each other to their feet. "Hurry and close the door, Florie," Elise said. "It's dry in here. Can ye believe it?" She walked around the circumference of the massive room, not finding any sign of leaks anywhere. A healthy share of dust, cobwebs, filth, and broken furniture, but no water at all. She stopped in front of the large hearth situated between a pair of shadowy archways. One led to a stair, and near as she could tell, the other opened into a hallway leading to the wing she thought might hold the kitchen. With one hand propped on the large stones of the hearth, she peered up into the darkness of the chimney. "I hope it draws, or we'll have a room full of smoke."

"I've got my tinderbox ready, m'lady." Florie joined her, then glanced back at the heart of the room. "Might as well burn those broken chairs." She tipped her head, waiting for permission to gather what she had in mind. "Dry wood, ye ken?"

Elise agreed. "Yes. We'll get a good fire going in here, then see what secrets the place holds."

"Aye." The maid hurried to gather the broken furniture scattered around the room and piled in the corners. "We'll get a good fire going in every hearth we can find. Warm this place up in no time."

It took them a little while, but soon they not only enjoyed a roaring fire in the main room but also both hearths on the second floor, and the hearth and sheltered cooking pit of the attached kitchen. The third floor of the tower proved to be a disappointment. A cloying dampness paired with a strong musty odor hinted at thatching in dire need of repair. The hearth worked well enough since it was a part of the chimney system from below, but even a crackling fire had no effect on the puddles spreading across the floor. Buckets fetched by the pair of lads Ross sent to help them managed the wetness and kept it from seeping through to the second floor. With any hope, a constant roaring fire would dry out the rest until they repaired their roofing.

With a swipe of her hand across her brow, Elise surveyed all they had accomplished so far. There was more to be done than one day could manage, especially since they had arrived after midday. But at least the neglect and damage had been far less dramatic than she feared. Shorter days, the weariness of the

MAEVE GREYSON

trying journey, and a demanding growl of her stomach, pointed her to the next priority. Everyone needed a hearty, hot meal.

She had finally found a purpose for her life—for now.

"All will be needing to eat," she told Florie as she leaned her broom against the wall and headed toward the kitchens.

"Want I should help?" The maid paused in sweeping down cobwebs. "The lads can finish in here, then mind the other floors."

"Aldis? Elliott? I trust ye both know all that's needed?" Elise gave the young lads an encouraging yet stern nod. They had stayed busy so far, but now they had the chance to prove what they could do when no one watched them.

"Aye, m'lady." Aldis gave her a wide grin, then dumped another armload of firewood beside the main hearth to dry.

"I can outwork that one any day," Elliott bragged with a good-natured cut of his eyes at Aldis. "We'll get this place cleaned and the rest of the furniture brought in afore ye can think twice about it."

"Work well, my fine lads, and I'll see that ye get extra supper and a good word in the commander's ear for yer troubles." That seemed to increase their enthusiasm. She just prayed they didn't do more harm than good with their rough and tumble antics while they worked.

As she walked through the low-ceilinged hallway to the kitchens, she wished she had brought her broom. This tunnel-like area hadn't been cleaned yet, and she counted at least three dried mouse carcasses along the walls. Thankfully, these were long dead, but that meant the live ones lurked in the shadows. She made a mental note to ask Ross if they might get a cat or two. One for here and one for the stable. The closer she drew to the kitchens, the more her steps slowed. That smell. Rich. Juicy. Mouth-watering. As if the kitchen had come to life and started cooking on its own since everyone else was busy. Her stomach rumbled, urging her forward.

She pushed through the rickety door hanging by one hinge

64

and stopped.

"Turn it, man," Ross shouted through the open double doors on the other end of the long, narrow kitchen. "I can smell the char, and I dinna relish burnt meat."

Elise blinked, unable to believe her eyes. The surly, scowling provisions knave who had snapped at Florie the entire journey had disappeared. With his dark hair slicked back in a neat queue and an apron lashed around his waist, Munro grinned from ear to ear as he turned the massive spit over the roasting pit just outside the double kitchen doors. A thatched roof and two walls sheltered the area from the weather, while its open end and wide windows allowed the smoke to billow up and out rather than back into the kitchen. A good-sized carcass sizzled and popped over the fire, its skin crisping nicely with the help of whatever the knave basted across it between its turnings.

Ross also wore an apron and stood at the worktable beside the hearth, chopping root vegetables and tossing them into a round-bellied pot hung over the fire. He tossed a glance back at a pair of young lads working dough at another table. "We need to be starting those bannocks, ye ken? The hearth oven should be hot enough by now."

Elise moved deeper into the controlled chaos of the delicious-smelling room. A kitchen full of men? The master of the house, even? 'Twas madness.

"Ye cook?" she asked when Ross looked her way.

He grinned. "Aye, I enjoy it. 'Tis Munro's job as my provisions knave, but I've always given him a hand because I found it relaxes me."

"Where did the game come from?" Not only did meat turn on the spit, but three skillets on the board beside the window held large, plucked carcasses of some kind of fowl. "Ye didn't kill our stock, did you? We must grow our herd before we take from them."

"Dinna fash yerself, m'love." He pecked a light kiss on her cheek as he edged past to get several large onions from a sack hanging in a small, recessed larder. "Valan and Niall went on a hunt. Got us that fine deer and those pheasants." He picked up another small sack and tucked it in the crook of his arm. "And ye'll be pleased to know, all yer wee beasties are bedded down, nice and warm in the barracks. They've had their grass, their grain, and fresh water. Tomorrow, I'll send the lads foraging for more fodder since the MacDougall didna spare us enough to suit me."

Unable to resist, she stirred the bubbling cauldron and wafted the steam toward her nose. "Onions and barley to come, I suppose? And plenty of black pepper and salt?"

"We willna need the salt. I didna rinse the packed fish all that much, so the stew will be plenty briny enough even with the barley and greens." He gave her a sly tip of his head. "And I'll thank ye to not question my cooking, dear wife. Ye should count yerself fortunate to have such a talented husband." The way he stressed the word talented made it clear he spoke of more than artfulness in the kitchen.

Her cheeks, as well as other places, warmed without aid of a fire. "I consider myself verra blessed." She daren't say anymore. Not in front of the lads filling trays with lumps of dough that would soon become delicious buns to sop in the gravies and stews. She backed toward the door, still unable to tear her gaze from the unusual kitchen staff. "I shall see that Aldis and Elliott have the table and benches inside and dried off. Those two are quite the workers, by the way. They deserve extra supper."

"I'm proud to hear it." Ross didn't look up from chopping the onions. "They'll probably stay on with us here. They're both too slight for campaigns."

"What about archery?" She'd overheard Aldis's wistful mention of joining the *Gallóglaigh* someday.

Ross paused and tilted his head as if mulling over the suggestion, then shrugged and went back to chopping. "If they can prove themselves good enough to pass Adellis's tests, I'm sure Thorburn would welcome them." He gave her a kindly smile.

"But as commander of a single unit, I can only suggest and advise. As constable, Thorburn has the final say."

"I will tell them to practice when they can." She hoped the boys would make it. Hopes and dreams were such precious things. She hated to see anyone disappointed.

"Elise."

Ross's call halted her just as she pushed open the door to leave. "Yes?"

"Have them see to our bedchamber, aye?" The meaningful quirk of his smile made her catch her breath. "After supper, I would hold my wife and christen our new home properly, ye ken?"

She caught her lip between her teeth, dipped a quick nod, then turned and hurried away, finding the kitchen entirely too warm. Only a few hours ago, she'd been cold as ice floating in the sea. Not now. She grabbed her neckline and fluttered it, trying to move some air across her heated flesh.

Florie met her at the archway. "We've the table and benches set and dried. Extra benches and chairs were brought in too. The lads are fetching in all the trunks now." She paused to take a breath and frowned. "Ye look quite red in the face, m'lady. Are ye unwell?"

Elise's cheeks felt hot to the touch, and she knew why. She fanned herself while at the same time waving away Florie's concerns. "I'm quite well. Just came from the kitchen." She stepped closer and lowered her voice. "I found yer Master Munro smiling."

The maid's dark brows rose to her hairline. "Impossible. Are ye sure that surly goat's face wasna cracked, and ye mistook it for a smile?"

Elise shook her head, relieved to have veered Florie's attention away from herself. "The man was as pleased as could be, turning a fine fat venison on the spit." She gave a knowing dip of her chin as she snatched up her broom and started up the stairs. "And Commander Ross was chopping onions and carrots.

Already had a stew bubbling on the hearth."

Florie cleared her throat and gave a disbelieving look. "Me thinks ye have a fever to have such visions. Shall I make a poultice for ye, m'lady?"

Clapping a hand over her heart, Elise smiled as she bumped the door open with her hip. "I swear on my heart. 'Tis every bit of it true." She went silent at what met her on the second floor.

Florie beamed a smug look as she marched across the chamber. "Why whatever's wrong, m'lady?"

"When was this done?" Elise eased forward, then crouched down and ran her fingers across the thick weave of a dark blue tapestry bordered with red flowers entwined with leaves of gold. "It's not the wee bit damp. How is that possible?"

For once, Florie assumed a rare silence, sashaying around the room as if to direct Elise's gaze to the comfortable furnishings. A massive, canopied bed. Trunks. A pair of wardrobes. Tables. Candelabras on the mantel. A couch on one end of the chamber, its surface covered with pillows and cushions.

"Florie? When? And how is it all dry as can be?"

Unable to stay quiet any longer, Florie lit up with a wide smile. "Commander had them wrap everything good and snug in oiled tent cloth before they packed it in the trunks and wardrobes. There is a bit of dampness, but if we keep the fire roaring, 'twill be gone before ye know it."

"Is this what ye and the lads kept bumping and whispering about while I scrubbed the floors?"

Florie grinned again. "Aye. That's why Elliott took so long in coming to help ye dump the buckets of filthy water. He and Aldis liked to never got the wardrobes up the stairs without ye seeing. That's when I took ye to the root cellar to see if it was dry enough to bring in the barrels of vegetables and fruit."

"I wondered by ye kept me down there so long." Tears welled in her eyes and overflowed before she could catch them. She spun about and dashed them away, ashamed at revealing how Florie and the lads had touched her heart.

"M'lady?" Florie cleared her throat again. "M'lady? Did we err in setting up yer rooms without yer overseeing it? Did we overstep?"

Without turning to face the maid, Elise bowed her head. "No, Florie. The boys and yerself did such a lovely job I couldna bear the joy of it. Forgive me."

"So, ye're happy then?" the maid asked with a hesitant leeriness that threatened to make Elise cry even more.

She turned and took hold of the girl's hands. "I am happier than I have been in a verra long while. The lot of ye did a fine job. 'Tis absolutely perfect."

"Thank goodness." Florie blew out a breath as though she'd held it overlong. "We had help, ye ken? Aldis got some of the other lads to join in, so's we'd get done all the quicker."

Her gaze lit on the flickering candles, the cheery fire in the hearth, and the furnishings fit for the Lord of Argyll himself. Joy filled her, but fear and dread chased close behind. All could disappear even quicker than it came. And if it lasted 'til spring, how could she find the strength to leave it?

"What do ye wish to do next, m'lady?" Florie stepped directly in front of her, thankfully interrupting her melancholy. The bubbly maid's wide smile lit the room brighter than the candles. "Since the master's solar be done, what's next?"

"The other room on this floor, has anything been done with it?" Elise studied the size of the current chamber, estimating that it took up most of the second floor.

Florie shook her head. "We didna ken what ye wished done with it." With a dip of her chin, she smirked a knowing grin. "'Course we figured it to be a nursery soon enough."

Florie's eerie ability to see into her most secret dreams disturbed her, so she didn't grace that comment with a reaction. "Fetch the boys and have them help ye set it up for yer own room. After all, ye can't be sleeping down in the hall with all the men." Elise turned toward the door. "Come. Let's see what needs to be done for ye to have a place to lay yer weary head this evening."

CHAPTER SIX

"WHY, ELISE?" ROSS trailed his hand across her bare shoulder and down her arm as she lay curled against him. "We agreed to be man and wife through winter, and we get along well. I dinna understand how ye can still talk about spring and leaving as if ye canna wait for that time?" He raised up a bit and pressed a lingering kiss to her forehead. "I would have us be man and wife the rest of our lives. Why do ye not feel the same? What makes ye so unhappy here?"

Here it was, almost Hogmanay, and yet every now and again, she still mentioned leaving, even though she seemed contented and pleased at Tórrelise. Life wasn't easy here by any means, but it was a damn sight better than what she might face should she insist on leaving. "Why must ye hold so tight to the notion of going away?" It not only confused him but made the middle of his chest ache with a pain he couldn't bear.

She remained silent for so long, he wondered if her stubbornness refused to allow an answer. Just as he thought to nettle her again, she lifted her head and spoke.

"If I let myself embrace this life ye have given me," she paused, eased in a deep breath, and slowly released it. "If I claim it for my own and cherish it, something will happen." She settled back down in the crook of his arm, nestling her cheek against his chest.

"What do ye mean, something will happen?" After an enormous meal, plenty of whisky, and a fine hearty romp on the couch, then another in the bed, his ability to counter any argument she made had somewhat dulled. "What could happen?" he repeated, determined to end this talk of her someday leaving before they closed their eyes. Though he had sworn never to love after his father's death, fate had changed that somehow. He had a wife to love and protect now, and he'd be damned if he wouldn't fight to keep her.

"I am cursed," she admitted, cuddling tighter and draping an arm and leg across him. "Fate will take ye away from me if I'm foolish enough to believe this..." She flipped a hand as if encompassing both him and the room. "I canna fall into that trap. This happiness can never be mine forever."

"Fate brought ye to me, did it not?" He rubbed his eyes with his free hand, struggling to come up with the words to reason away her fear. He understood why she felt as she did but did not know how to make it go away.

"Naught but temptation," she explained, her tone solemn and hopeless. "A trick to make the pain more difficult to bear when it snatches ye away."

"But if ye hold steadfast to yer plan and leave come spring, then ye think Fate will leave ye be?" That made no sense at all to him, but it did to her, and that was all that mattered. Even when she didn't speak about leaving, he saw it in her eyes. Always there. Those shadows haunted her. "Ye think that's what Fate wishes?"

"Aye. 'Tis the only way to keep ye safe from any ill-tidings." She blew out another heavy sigh that tickled across his chest hairs. "Why does it vex ye so? It's not as if ye ever need to worry about being alone. Another will come along within hours of my leaving. Ye know yer bed will never be cold."

He rolled her to her back and rose above her, clamping hold of her wrists and burying them into the pillows. Locking his gaze with hers, he pressed so close that her breathing tickled across his face. "I dinna want another woman. I want ye." He settled down between her legs and worked his hips, nudging her to prove his point. "Does that feel as if I want another woman?"

"Yer cock loves any warm, wet place. It doesna give a damn which woman provides it." The sadness in her eyes as she curled a leg around him gave him pause. "I dinna mind though. Ye always give me wondrous pleasure."

With a frustrated huff, he rolled off her, left their bed, and strode over to the hearth. She deserved happiness. Why couldn't she see that? He thumped his fist against the mantel and leaned into it, staring down at the orange-red heat rippling through the coals. Perhaps she *should* leave come spring if she couldn't allow herself to accept him. But that very thought battered him like a spiked mace smashing into his chest.

"It's not that I'm ungrateful," she called to him from the bed.

He turned and glared at her. "I dinna want yer damned gratitude, woman. I want yer love."

A dark silence fell between them. It gnashed its teeth and ridiculed him for his inability to change her heart and her mind. When she didn't respond, he threw himself into a chair in front of the hearth and dropped his head into his hands, scrubbing his face to keep from growling out his frustrations and frightening her.

The Lord of Argyll and O'Conor had bested him after all. Joined him to a woman who would never love him. But that wasn't what hurt. Those fools could all be damned. The pain and irony of his false marriage ripped his heart from his chest. He had never loved any woman he had ever bedded. Until now. And this precious lass rejected him. Not for another man. Or for God. But because of superstitions she had endured. He was at a loss, doomed to lose her, and he hated himself for it.

Her soft touch on his back made his muscles flinch into harder knots. He had no words, so he didn't bother lifting his head from his hands. The chair creaked as she sat on its padded arm. She slid her hand across his shoulders and rested her cheek against his back.

"Go to bed, lass," he ordered quietly. "Apparently, we have

no more to say about this subject."

"Forgive me for upsetting ye," she whispered with a gentle tucking of his hair behind his ear. "But ye know what I say is true. It is for the best."

Such an unreasonable excuse infuriated him. He slid out from under her and stood, causing her to tumble into the chair. His body ratcheted so taut and ready to fight for her love, he shuddered. With a hard jerk, he turned and jabbed a finger at her. "It is not for the best! Ye made me love ye, damn ye. How can yer leaving me be for the best? The not knowing if ye live or die or what wickedness might happen to ye? How is that the best for me?" He stabbed the air again. "I swore to protect ye because I cared about what happened to ye. That caring turned into a fondness that grew into love. And now—now all that caring has done is brought me pain because ye willna even attempt to love me back." He pounded his fist on his chest. "I love ye, dammit, and I have never said that to any woman. Not ever. And yet ye willna even try to care for me the slightest bit."

Tears welled in her amber eyes, and her bottom lip quivered. Without breaking their locked stares, she clambered out of the seat and jabbed a finger right back at him. "I dinna have to try and love ye because I already do, damn ye! And it scares the living hell out of me. All I have ever loved, all I have ever cherished, has always been taken from me. I canna bear to lose ye. Can ye not understand that? If any ill befalls ye, they might as well bury me with ye." Her tears overflowed, making her cheeks shimmer in the firelight. "I canna bear it. Just kill me now so I might know peace rather than live in fear for when the evil comes to take ye away because of me."

He yanked her into his arms and crushed her to his chest. "Nothing in life is promised to last forever," he rasped into her hair. "All we can do is hold tight to what we have while we have it."

She clutched him just as tightly, baptizing him with her tears. "But what if—"

"We canna live our lives in fear of *what if*. If we do, we will never live at all." He swept her up into his arms and sat them in the chair. No sleep would be had until she understood and swore to stay. "I know ye have suffered, but I also know ye've got the courage and fire to spit at the past and grab hold of every happiness that comes yer way just to spite the bastards. Dinna run and cower in fear just to survive. Laugh, dance, do whatever makes ye happy, and then thrive, Elise. *Thrive*. That is the greatest revenge." He smoothed her hair back and tipped her face up to his. "Will ye at least try? For me and my heart's sake?"

"Never leave me," she whispered, her eyes shimmering with her tears. "Please?"

"I will do my damnedest to never leave ye," he promised. "If ye swear to do the same for me."

"I will."

"Swear it." He leaned closer 'til the tip of his nose almost touched hers.

A hint of a smile quirked a corner of her mouth. "I swear I will never leave ye. No matter the season."

He kissed her long and hard, pouring all his relief, all his hopes, and dreams into her. God help them both. She feared love, and so did he, but here they were, so stricken with the powerful emotion, they could hardly bear it.

"We are a pitiful pair, we are," she said as she shifted in his arms and straddled him.

A low rumbling laugh escaped him as he slid his hands up and down the smoothness of her back, then cupped her bottom that had filled out and rounded to a delicious handful over the past few months. "And like-minded at last." He breathed in her scent, the sweetness of her hair, the fruitiness of the wine still on her lips, and the enticing fragrance of a woman well-loved and about to be loved again. "Shall I carry ye to our bed?" he offered.

"No. Ye shall have me here, my husband." She lifted herself up, reached down between them, and placed his cock right where it belonged. "There now," she murmured as she settled down on him. "How is that?"

He arched upward to ensure she was seated to the hilt. "Perfection, m'love." The joints of the chair creaked in a not-so-subtle warning. With one hand cupping her breast and the other squeezing her fine behind, he rocked his hips upward again. "And my body loves ye as much as my soul does. It wants no other. Why else would it hunger for ye again and again, no matter how many times we've loved?"

Holding on to his shoulders, she rode with a slow steady rhythm, then gave him a wicked smile. "Since I have nothing to compare ye to, I reckon ye're the best I have ever had."

"Such shamelessness must be punished." He lunged upward, keeping himself buried in her warm, wet nest as he picked her up and laid her down on the furs in front of the hearth. With a tauntingly slow thrust, he ground in deep, then pulled out.

"Faster," she breathed, lifting her legs to dig her heels into his buttocks and pull him forward.

"Nay, my love. I'll not pound to the finish until ye canna bear my stroking any longer."

She bucked beneath him, meeting him thrust for thrust. "I see I have married a wicked man."

"Aye, love." He slid in hard and ground his hips, loving the way she clenched her teeth and arched to rake her tightened nipples against his chest. "I am verra wicked when it comes to pleasing the woman I love."

"And I am verra thankful." She raked her fingernails down his back, latched hold of his buttocks, and pulled. "But if ye dinna get a move on, I shall die." Her breath came quick, and her heartbeat twitched on the side of her lovely throat. She yanked him forward again. "By all that's holy, give me what I need. I beg ye."

"I dinna want yer begging," he rasped, struggling with his own control. He thrust in deep again and held. "I want yer love. Forever."

"Ye have it." She closed her eyes and arched again. "I swear."

"Then say it."

"I love ye, Ross MacDougall, with all my heart and soul. Now move, damn ye! Move!"

"Gladly, m'lady, gladly." Never would he be accused of denying his lady love her wishes. As she shuddered and groaned his name, he pounded harder, roaring his own release until he collapsed atop her.

They lay there, gasping to catch their breath. The fire popped, sending a burning ember dangerously close.

"We best tend to the fire and move, else we get singed," she murmured in a lazy tone that assured him he had pleased his lady well.

As much as he hated to end their connection, he pecked a kiss to her forehead and pushed himself to his feet. With the fire iron, he tamed the fire back under control, added wood, then brushed the cinders off the furs and back onto the hearthstone. "Perhaps while in the village tomorrow we should check with the smithy for something to block the sparks."

"Ye wish me to go with ye?" Elise rose to her feet and stretched, the beauty of her nakedness making him want her all over again. When she relaxed and noticed her effect on him, she arched a brow. "We should sleep now if ye plan to leave out early."

"I canna help it." He pulled her into a hug, swept her into his arms, and took her to their bed. "But ye are right, m'love. I shall strive to control my ardor—at least for the rest of tonight." He climbed in beside her, pulled her close, and gathered the bedclothes up over them. "And yes, I thought ye might like to come to the village. Ye've nay been anywhere since we settled here."

"It's not as if I've had nothing to do," she defended, settling into her usual spot in the dip of his shoulder. With her arm and leg across him, she gave a contented sigh. "There's always something to be done, but that's a good thing. We are verra blessed."

"That we are." He closed his eyes and curled his arm tighter around her. "Florie and the lads can look after the place whilst we're gone. 'Twill only be for a day."

"Even traveling by sledge?"

"Aye, the settlement's closer than ye think. Argyll land. Their fealty belongs to the MacDougall, so ye'll find us more than a little welcome there since I am a *Gallóglaigh* commander."

"As long as I am with ye, that's welcome enough for me."

Ross smiled. At last. She dared to embrace their future. As he drifted off into oblivion, he prayed it would last.

⟫⟩⟨⟨

EVEN THOUGH THE wind nipped with an icy bite, the brilliance of the blue sky and the sunshine sparkling across the snow made it a perfect day for a quick jaunt across the glen. Ross rode alongside them, sometimes taking the lead. His shaggy beast's great hairy feet kicked up the white fluff with every step, leaving snowy smoke in its wake.

Elliott drove the sledge. Aldis and Florie stayed behind to ensure the others helping to restore the place did as they should while their master and mistress were away.

Elise lifted her face to the sun, not caring that her cheeks and the tip of her nose burned with the cold. It was a glorious day, and she intended to do as Ross had begged her. This day and every day thereafter, she would embrace the goodness while it lasted and thrive to spite all who had treated her ill.

"I see smoke from the village chimneys, m'lady," Elliott said with a nod toward a rise that almost hid a line of pines. He pointed to the darkest column of gray spiraling to the east of the other smoky spires. "See that one right there? That be the smithy's fire. It always blows the darkest smoke of any."

"Well, are ye not the canny lad. I never knew that." She shielded her eyes from the glare and peered at the several spikes of smoke climbing into the blue beyond the trees. Every house and shop would have a fire to stave off the December day's chill.

"My da was a smithy." Elliott's smile tightened, then faded as he squinted at the path ahead. "Afore I came to Argyll. I used to help him some."

She didn't have to ask. The mourning in Elliott's tone was plain as the beard on his chin. "I am sorry, Elliot."

The lad shrugged away her condolences and snapped the reins. "He died doing what he loved." His mouth quivered as he battled his emotions. "Forge blew up on him. Killed him outright." He shrugged again. "Least he didna suffer a slow journey to the other side."

She rested a hand on his arm. "He is watching over ye, Elliott, and I know he's prouder than proud. Ye're a fine lad. The verra finest."

With an embarrassed smile, he tucked his chin. His cheeks flamed a deeper red than the icy breeze had already chapped them. "I thank ye, m'lady."

Since the snow wasn't deep at all, the packed trail into the small village of Creagnarloch led them over the ridge and through the trees. The settlement was comprised of two long rows of sturdy, two-story buildings with snow-covered rooftops stained gray from the smoke billowing out of their chimneys. A smattering of thatch-covered wattle and daub houses dotted the surrounding landscape.

Ross motioned to the end of the lane that lay but a few paces from them. "Elliott, speak with the smithy about guards for all the hearths. Ye know well enough what we should pay and whether the man knows his craft." He dismounted and tied the reins of his mount to the back of the sledge. "My lady wife needs cloth and thread. Once we find what she needs, we'll meet ye at the pub and enjoy a whisky to warm us for the journey home."

Elliott hopped to the ground and secured the team to the post nearest the smithy's forge. "I'll see if the man has what ye need, m'lord. If he doesna have any on hand and his wares are good, shall I tell him ye wish him to make some to pick up later?"

"Aye." Ross pulled several coins from a leather pouch and placed them in the young man's hand. "We need at least two immediately. More when he can spare them." With a curt nod, he clapped Elliott's shoulder. "A good price, mind ye."

"The best, m'lord." Elliott winked and headed inside.

Ross turned back and offered her his arm. "Ye have a sparkle to yer eyes, m'love. Is it the cold that suits ye or the trip?"

"It's everything." She hugged closer as they walked to the center building, the one with its small windows all aglow and hand-painted signs hinting at the finery within. "But mostly, it's my life that has me so happy."

"Life?" He quirked a blonde brow as he ushered her to the door.

"Are ye fishing, my love?" she teased.

He opened the door for her. "And what if I am?" With an expectant arch of a brow, he brushed the snow off her skirts before she stepped inside.

"Then ye should know I am happy because I love ye." She would gladly tell him what he wished to hear. She would shout it from the rooftops if he asked.

With a satisfied smugness, he puffed out his chest and closed the door behind them. "Aye, then. That is what I wished to hear."

"Well, well, do my eyes deceive me? Is that Ross MacDougall?" The voice came from the other side of the room. Behind a low table in front of shelves filled with colorful rolls of cloth and spools of ribbon and lace, a buxom woman with silky blonde hair and a narrow-eyed sneer sauntered out of the shadows and leaned across the table. Her tone dripped with a poisonous combination of seduction and hatred. "I heard ye married. Is it true? Is *that* yer wife?"

Ross drew closer and slid his arm around her waist, which Elise appreciated. She already knew she didn't like this woman, and a battle simmered slow and steady. A battle she refused to lose. This woman stank of jealousy and envy.

"Jennet Faust meet my lady wife, Elise MacDougall."

Elise gave a polite dip of her chin while ensuring her tone remained cold and aloof enough to ire the already angry woman even more. "A pleasure, Mistress Faust."

The surly shopkeeper responded with a disgusted huff and curled her painted lips to an uglier slant.

Ross nudged Elise forward and made a show of fingering a large roll of linen on a table beside the hearth. "Might this do for Florie?" He acted as if, now that the introductions had been made, the infuriating woman no longer mattered. "Was it linen ye needed for her?"

"That there's already sold." Mistress Faust snatched up the bolt and toted it to another shelf. After tossing it down, she brushed off her hands and glared at them. "There's nary a thing in my shop I'll sell to the likes of her." She gave Elise an up and down scowl, then snorted with another insulting huff.

Ross started forward, but Elise caught hold of his sleeve and stopped him. Before he could speak, she strode to the money table and plopped down the leather purse of coins with a loud rattle. "Now, that is poor business indeed, Mistress Faust. Cutting off yer nose to spite yer face? I doubt ye will have a shop long with that attitude."

"When he tires of humping yer skinny arse, he knows where to come for a real woman." The sour-faced woman slid her hands under her heavy breasts and lifted them until her nipples nearly popped out from the ruffles of her neckline. "I heard about ye. The whore with the devil's mark. Ye're the feckin' revenge for his cuckolding O'Conor and the MacDougall. A hearty jest they're still laughing about at Dunstaffnage. Ye're the joke of Argyll, in fact." Her large breasts jiggled as she tittered out a mean-spirited cackle. "He'll be back in my bed before Hogmanay. I'll bet my best silk on it."

"Woman or not, no one speaks to my wife in such a manner." Ross launched himself over the table, grabbed hold of Mistress Faust's arm, and walked her back to the shelves of cloth behind her. "Ye will not only apologize to my lovely wife, but ye will also sell her anything she wishes or Lady Christiana shall know of yer poisonous tongue. Ye should ken well enough that when her ladyship blackballs yer shop, no one will darken yer door ever again."

"Come, dear husband. We can make do with what we have until spring." Elise scooped up her purse and tied it back to her belt. "We shall visit the ports then and purchase whatever we wish."

Ross released the rude wench and then wiped his hand on a bolt of cloth as if touching her soiled him. He strode back and stood at Elise's side, filling her with such love and pride she feared she would surely burst.

Fueled by his show of love and support, she leaned forward and locked eyes with the insolent shopkeeper. "Mistress Faust can shove every roll of cloth in this shop up her fat arse. Crossways."

"Bitch!" the woman screamed.

"Maybe so," Elise countered as she linked arms with Ross. "But I am the bitch with the husband."

Ross yanked open the shop door, setting the bell atop it jangling. He tossed a snarling glare back at Mistress Faust. "Good day to ye. I'm sure Lady Christiana will pay ye a visit after we see her at Hogmanay."

"Rot in hell! The both of ye!"

Without a glance back, Elise stepped out of the shop with her head held high.

Ross leaned in close. "Ye willna let that jealous wretch rattle ye, aye?"

"I will not." She felt strangely calm and not upset in the least. "I have what she wants. That is all that matters." However, she couldn't help but wonder how he had ever wanted a woman like that. Of course, she supposed men dreamed of suffocating in a lady's abundant cleavage, and that hateful hen had big enough breasts to kill several men at once. As they headed for the pub on the other side of the lane, she cast a side-eyed glance in his direction. "But I have to ask—why her? Was she not that vicious when ye bedded her?"

With a look akin to sheer terror, Ross shook his head and walked faster. "Nay, my lady love. Those sorts of questions are as dangerous as a hangman's noose." He patted her hand in the crook of his arm. "As ye said, we have each other now, and that is all that matters. Let the past remain in the past."

"Coward," she accused as they entered the pub, but softened it with a smile. "It is a shame about the cloth, though. She had some verra fine wares."

"As ye said, we'll take a trip to the port when the weather's milder and find everything we need." He pulled out her chair. "Have a seat, m'lady. We shall relax here in the warm and enjoy a drink while we wait for Elliott."

Elise seated herself, determined to enjoy the day even though her shopping quest had failed. She had never been *inside* a pub before. Hunted for scraps behind a few while on the run in Ireland. Even tried to get work in one, but the owner had laughed her out of the place, jeering that her face would scare away all his customers. She shoved the memories away. As Ross said, no more living in the past. Today was a treat. A fine trip with the man she loved. She held that thought close and concentrated on it.

"Commander Ross, how be ye?" the hefty barmaid asked as she thumped down a pair of glasses and a bottle of whisky. She gave Elise a friendly nod. "And this be yer lovely wife, I suppose?"

"Aye." Ross tossed a couple of coins on the table. "My lady love." He scooped up Elise's hand and kissed it.

The girl pushed the coins back toward Ross. "Nah. No money from ye today. Da says this is the least he owes ye. A wedding gift, ye ken?" She bobbed her head toward Elise again. "Congratulations, mistress. Fine man, ye married. Saved my da's life and helped him get this pub goin'."

"Thank ye. I consider myself verra fortunate to have found him." Elise flicked a hand to encompass the room. "And this is a fine pub indeed."

The maid glanced around the dimly lit establishment, then leaned closer. "Dinna let the others wear on ye. Bunch of cruel gossips, they are. But most are like me and Da. We be good people here in Creagnarloch, ye ken?"

Even though she had no idea what the young woman meant, Elise smiled. "I thank ye." As the girl sauntered away, Elise took notice of the other few customers scattered among the tables and sitting at the bar. All were men. All tossed repeated smirks in her direction. Then she understood the lass's comment. Apparently, Jennett Faust wasn't the only resident of Creagnarloch who knew of the Lord of Argyll and O'Conor's cruel jest. She clasped her hands in her lap and stared down at them.

"And what do we know is the best revenge, my love?" Ross leaned forward and tipped his head to peep up into her face. "We should pity the likes of these fools if their lives are so barren, they've nothing to amuse themselves with other than how we met." With a gentle nudge of his finger, he lifted her chin. "I love ye, Elise, and I am glad ye're my wife. All else can be damned."

"And I love ye." She touched his face, catching her breath when he turned his head and pressed a kiss into her palm.

"Ye're already here in the pub?" Elliott waved down the barmaid as he pulled up a chair. "It didna take ye long to select all the things they're loading onto the sledge. I figured ye still inside the shop the way they're still coming out with more."

"Loading?" Elise repeated, trying to understand the awe in Elliott's voice. "We bought nothing in that shop. It seemed our money wasna good enough for the keeper."

The lad shrugged, took a long, deep draught of his ale, then shook his head as he plunked it back to the table. "All I can tell ye is that a pair of boys flagged me down and asked if the sledge belonged to Commander MacDougall. When I told them it did, they started packing it. I had to lash the one fireguard the smithy had to the back of the seat to make room for all those bolts and barrels and parcels. 'Tis so full, it's nearly crunching down through the snow." He tossed up both hands and shrugged again.

"I dinna ken how they think they'll secure it all on there. I told them we didna have enough rope or tarps to cover such a hoard, and they said it didna matter. Their mistress ordered it done and told them to see it done proper, or there'd be hell to pay." His eyes flared wide, and he jerked a contrite nod. "Beggin' yer pardon, m'lady. Forgive me for using such coarse language."

Ross scooted around and wiped the frost from the window. He squinted outside, leaning closer and wiping the window again as it fogged. The longer he peered out the window, the wider his smile grew. A low chuckle rumbled from him as he turned back around and faced the table. "It appears Mistress Faust had a change of heart, m'love." With a wink at Elliot, he leaned forward and propped his forearms on the table. "The sledge is quite full, and yet they load even more. I also spotted a folded tarp and a coil of new rope ready to secure it."

Elise itched to run outside and inspect the load but knew it wouldn't look proper. She leaned forward and lowered her voice. "Why would she do that?"

"Because, my love, while the Lord of Argyll might rule this part of Scotland, it is his wife who everyone respects and fears."

"Aye," Elliott said with a wide-eyed nod. "Everyone knows Lady Christiana is generous and kind to all. But if ye dare make her angry, ye best make yer peace with God because by the time her ladyship's done with ye, there willna be anything left to pray over."

"I'm grateful she feels kindly toward ye," she told Ross.

He shook his head. "Nay, m'love. She barely tolerates me. It's yerself she's taken under her wing." He held up his glass in a toast. "It appears ye have a powerful ally."

Elise raised her glass, touched it to his, and prayed he was right. It never hurt to have a powerful ally.

CHAPTER SEVEN

"**I** DINNA KEN what to do, Valan." Ross stole a glance around the main gathering room to ensure no one sat close enough to overhear the conversation. "The ewes are lambing fine and healthy. She picked one up, cradled it in her arms, and started crying." He shook his head, a sense of helplessness making him clench his teeth. "And wouldna say a word about what was wrong. Only stood there. Tears streaming down her cheeks."

As soon as the others helping in the lambing shed noticed, they fled. The cowards left him there with an inconsolable wife. And no matter what he said or did, she shook her head, cuddled the tiny lamb closer, and softly wept into its wool.

"Ye had to have done something." Valan eyed him as if he lied. "Or said something. That's how Thorburn always gets in trouble with Adellis."

"I swear I have done nothing but been the best of husbands." He crossed himself and shot a glance upward. "May God strike me down if that's nay the truth of it."

Valan rolled his eyes and took another swig of his ale. "All I can tell ye is ye're asking the wrong brother. I know nothing of wives, and I've damn sure never claimed to understand women."

Florie and Elise emerged from the stairwell and strode across the room at a hurried pace, heading for the new door leading to where they planned to plant the herb garden as soon as the ground warmed enough. Late February to early March was till a mite too early to set out the shoots the women had nurtured in the warm dampness of the kitchen windows. But within a few weeks, they planned to transplant the hardier greens outside.

"She does seem a mite…" Valan frowned. "Troubled," he finished. He slanted his mug toward Florie. "And that one there looks worried about her." He raised his tankard higher as though toasting his brilliance. "There lies the answer to yer questions, brother. Talk to her maid."

Ross fisted his hands on the table as he watched them exit the room. "I dinna ken if she'll tell me anything. Florie's loyal to a fault when it comes to Elise."

"Then get Munro to ask her." Valan waved down a lad carrying a pitcher and held up his glass for a refill.

"Why Munro?"

Frowning as if he couldn't believe his ears, Valan stared at him. "Are ye blind? The man's addled with her."

"He's sweet on Florie?"

"Aye." His brother belched and scratched his stomach. "Was there any of that bread left from breakfast?"

"Munro is sweet on Florie?" Ross repeated, determined to keep Valan's mind on the problem at hand rather than his stomach. "They fight like a pair of rams after the same ewe." Never could he remember the two ever sharing a civil word between them. Florie nagged, and Munro snarled. That was the only way they communicated.

Valan scrubbed a hand down his face and leaned across the table. "Remember Thorburn's old smithy and his woman?"

"Aye." Ross remembered that couple well. During one of their raging clashes, the woman had nearly skewered him with a fire iron she lobbed at her husband. "They fought like hell all the time. Still do, I reckon."

"Naw—dead now. Both of them. Fever took her first." Valan fixed Ross with a pointed look. "The smithy laid across her grave for days, sobbing and begging her to take him, too, until his sons came and dragged him away." He leaned closer. "The man died a sennight later."

"Took his own life or did the fever get him, too?"

Valan shook his head. "Just died. Sitting in his chair staring at the fire. Face all wet with tears. His boys swear the last thing he did right before he died was smile and say their mother's name."

"Ye think she came back for him? Their bond was that strong?"

With a shrug, Valan lifted his cup and emptied it. "All I know is they never shared a sweet word between them that anyone ever knew of. But he couldna live without her, and she loved him enough to come back and get him."

Ross pushed himself up from the table and swung his legs out from the bench. "I'm going to Munro. Ye watch the door, aye? If they come back in, come running and warn me."

"What about that bread?"

"Ye'll get yer feckin' bread when I'm done talking to Munro." He pointed at the door. "Watch it, or it's yer arse, ye ken?"

"I tell ye this—I am never marrying," Valan said loud enough for Ross to overhear as he charged away.

"Aye, well, I never thought to marry either, and yet here I am." Ross strode into the kitchen and came to a halt inside the door.

Munro stood at the long, low window with a shallow bowl of water. The burly man dipped his thick fingers into the liquid, then showered the tender young plants with droplets. When he spotted Ross, he hid the bowl behind his back and shuffled in place as though struggling to come up with a lie.

"I thought ye said ye'd be baking extra trenchers today?" Ross folded his arms across his chest and leaned against the doorpost.

"I am." Munro jutted his chin higher, making his curly black beard quiver. "Lady Elise asked for the plants to be watered."

"When?"

"As soon as I had time to get to it, she said." He shifted his weight from side to side. Water slopped out of the bowl, making him step aside and set it on the table. "Bugger." He scrubbed his boot across the puddle, grinding the water into the stone floor.

"Lady Elise hasna been in the kitchen today, but Florie has." Ross waited, giving the man enough rope to hang himself.

Munro's mustache twitched, and his dark eyes narrowed. "Lady Elise sent word by Florie. She does that now and again."

"I see." Ross took a step closer, and another.

Munro backed up a step. "Ye be needing something else, Commander?"

"Aye." Ross advanced again. "I need to know what Florie knows about my wife. Why has she been so upset lately?"

"Aw, hell no." Munro gave a vigorous shake of his head and turned away, busying himself at the bread table. "I canna help ye, m'lord. I wouldna know a feckin' thing about any of that."

"Ye canna lie worth a shite, man." That was one of the main reasons Ross trusted him so. Munro might be surly, insolent, and as hard to get along with as a sore-tailed badger, but the man was loyal, honest, and couldn't lie to save his soul. "What has Florie told ye?"

Munro remained silent, attacking the dough with a vengeance.

"Ye keep kneading it like that, and it'll be so tough even the animals canna eat it." With a glance back at the door, he stepped closer and lowered his voice. "I need to know why Lady Elise is so sad. What have I done to upset her?"

With a glance first at the door, then back at him, Munro shook his shaggy head again. "Florie'll have my arse."

"Who do ye fear most? Myself or Florie?"

"Florie." Munro swiped sweat from his brow, sprinkling flour down his nose and into his beard. "She's a damn site meaner than yerself, m'lord."

"If ye dinna tell me what I need to know, I'm going to tell Florie that ye always tell me everything she says." Ross smiled. He smelled victory at hand.

"Ye wouldna dare," Munro whispered. "Such a lie wouldna be Christian."

"I want my wife happy, and I will do whatever it takes to make her so."

Munro bared his teeth and punched the dough flat on the table. "Then get her with child." He jabbed a flour-covered fist in the air. "That is why she weeps. She fears she's barren."

"God's beard." Ross backed away as if the information shoved him. Of all the things he had feared her sadness to be, that they had yet to seed a child hadn't been one of them. He scrubbed a hand across his mouth and turned away. He should've known. As regular as the moon, her courses came every month. No matter how many times they loved. Yesterday, her bleeding had started right on schedule.

"Thank ye, Munro," he muttered. "And dinna fear. I willna say a thing to Florie."

"I am sorry, m'lord."

"As am I, Munro." Ross left the kitchen and returned to the table where Valan sat staring at the door.

"Where's my bread?" his brother asked after a sideways glance. Then he turned and gave Ross his full attention. "Ye've paled, brother. I take it ye now have yer answer."

Ross lowered himself to the bench and rubbed his forehead, wishing it would help him think of what to do. "Aye. I do have my answer."

"Can I help?" Valan leaned closer. "Who must I kill?"

"She fears she is barren." Ross bowed his head, cradling it between his hands. The news made his head pound as if he'd been drunk for a sennight.

"I canna help with that." Valan blew out a heavy sigh while rapping his knuckles on the table. "Ye've only been wed since last fall. Late September, aye?"

"Aye."

"That's naught but six months." His brother counted the months off on his fingers and finished with a firm nod. "Aye, six months. These things take time, ye ken? Ask Thorburn. I dinna think he got Adellis with child right away. It took nearly a year."

He scratched his chin and frowned. "At least, I think so anyway."

"It doesna matter what I think," Ross said. "What matters is what Elise fears." It had taken him months to talk her away from her superstitions about Fate stealing him from her. This could set her back. He knew in his heart she believed her lack of a child was some sort of punishment. Another way for Fate to torment her.

Valan eyed him, then reached across the table and gave his arm a consoling thump. "All I can say is ye best be laying with yer wife every chance ye get."

"Ye're a great help, brother." Ross scrubbed his face again. A heaviness settled in his chest, and his gut churned. What if something was wrong with his seed? After all, as many women as he'd known, not a one had ever gotten with child. He'd often counted himself lucky and blessed. Now, he wondered if his lack of illegitimate bairns might actually be a curse. Perhaps he was the one who was barren.

The door opened, and in walked Elise and Florie. His precious wife's gaze found him. Her steps slowed, and she gifted him with a gentle nod and a sad smile. His heart ached for her. How could he promise her all would be well when it came to this? If it were up to him, they would fill this place with children. But this—this was in God's hands.

Valan rose and clapped him on the shoulder. "I am off to find that bread."

Ross knew very well it wasn't hunger driving his brother away, but he could do little to stop him since Elise was almost upon them. He forced a smile and nodded toward the garden door. "Did the lads make the plot big enough? If not, I can have them turn more earth. They're due to work in the straw and manure later after they've finished cleaning the stable."

"I feel it will be fine for the herbs and such." She sat on the bench beside him, her tensed back facing the table and her hands folded in her lap. "Of course, we shall need another plot for vegetables. 'Tis a shame there's not enough room off the kitchen for either of the gardens. Whenever we wish for fresh herbs or greens, we'll either have to cross the main hall or go around the broch on the outside."

Ross spun his empty tankard between his hands, knowing full well that neither of them gave a rat's arse about the placement of the garden plots. This silly conversation served as a cushion of words between them, keeping them from the troublesome worry hanging over their heads like a storm cloud. He decided to address the issue as directly as she would allow. "As long as I have ye in my life, Elise, I am a happy man." He turned and fixed her with a steady look. "I dinna need anything other than you. Not riches. Not land." He paused and drew up the last of his courage. "Not children."

Her gaze fell to her hands. She stared at her whitened knuckles, while the muscles in her jaw worked with her clenching teeth. "That is good to know," she answered quietly. After another long, painful moment of silence, she rose and shook the wrinkles from her apron. "I have chores to attend to, m'lord, and then I think I shall rest until supper." Her composure close to breaking, she managed a strained smile. "I would appreciate it if ye'd do me the kindness of ensuring no one disturbs me. A weariness nags at me today."

He rose, took her hands in his, and kissed them. "I will see to it, m'lady." When she started to pull away, he held her fast. "I love ye, Elise." He wished he could pour all he felt into those three simple words, but he didn't know how. "Love ye more than ye will ever know."

A faint smile danced across her lips, but the light remained vacant from her eyes. "I love ye as well, my Ross." Then she eased her hands free and hurried away before he could stop her.

He stared after her, feeling utterly useless. Out of the corner of his eye, he caught a scurrying through the shadows. The small dark form moved again where the wall joined the floor. Another feckin' mouse. Munro had nearly dismantled the kitchen the other day while attempting to kill one with a pot and a broom. Then he remembered a request Elise had made when they first settled at the keep. A cat. She asked if they might get a cat for the tower and another for the stable. He rubbed his jaw as she disappeared up into the stairwell. Perhaps a cat would lift her spirits. He remembered his mother laughing at the playful antics of kittens born to a stable cat one spring.

Armed with hope and a plan that he prayed wouldn't fail, he charged out the main door and scanned the grounds. "Elliott! Aldis!"

Both young men halted their leveraging of a large block, freshly chiseled by the stonemason, toward the gap in the skirting wall. With the wooden pools held taut, they twisted to face him. "Aye, m'lord?" Aldis responded, sounding a mite out of breath.

"I've a different task for the both of ye. One of great importance. Hand that job off to someone else and meet me in the kitchen." Without a look back, Ross spun about and returned inside. When he gave orders, he expected them followed, whether it be in his home or on the battlefield.

"Valan!" His shout boomed to the rafters. "Kitchen. Now."

Valan scooped up his bread in one hand, his tankard of ale in the other, and charged toward the kitchen as if going to war.

Startled by the sudden onslaught, Munro grabbed a mallet in one hand and a cleaver in the other. "Who dares attack us?"

"No one," Ross said, motioning Valan, Aldis, and Elliott to step closer. "I've chosen the three of ye to join me in a sacred mission."

"Aye?" Valan tossed his bread into the fire, downed his drink, then thumped the empty tankard onto the sideboard. He pounded a fist to his chest. "Name it, and it shall be done."

Aldis and Elliot leaned in, their focus riveted.

Munro joined the group. "Count me in as well, m'lord. I willna fail ye."

"Munro, I need ye here to maintain order and keep Lady Elise and Florie from discovering anything might be amiss, ye ken?" Ross gave the man a stern look to drive the order home.

Munro nodded. "Aye, m'lord. 'Twill be done."

Ross turned to the other three. "Before this day ends, we must find at least two cats. One for the tower. One for the stable. And if we find kittens, we shall bring back the entire litter. Along with the mother cat as well." He charged them to know the urgency. "More than a pair of cats willna hurt a thing. We shall see this done, ye ken?"

"Cats," Valan repeated. He straightened and took a step back, eyeing Ross as if he'd just ordered them to eat horse shite. "Are ye drunk?" He tossed a glance back at his empty tankard and scowled at the fire. "I burned my bread because ye think the keep needs cats?"

"Lady Elise mentioned she would like a cat or two." Ross glared at his brother, willing him to understand and say no more. Entirely too many already knew of his lady love's woes. Neither Aldis nor Elliott needed that information.

Valan's mouth flattened into a terse line. "And where shall we search for these cats?"

"Tame or feral?" Aldis asked.

"Are ye daft? He'll want'm tame, so they'll stay here." Elliott rolled his eyes.

"Feral hunts better," Aldis defended. "Better mousers, my mam always said."

With one hand clapped on Aldis's shoulder and the other on Elliott's, Valan grinned. "It appears we have experts, dear brother. What a fortunate bunch of buggers we are."

"Valan." Ross glared at him, daring him to make one more snide remark. "Lady Elise wants cats. Cats she shall have."

"Aye, m'lord." Valan's grin faded, and he adjusted his stance to a more respectful posturing. Eyes narrowed, his head tilted as he appeared to be deep in thought. "What about the miller? With all that grain, he's sure to keep cats to control the vermin."

Ross nodded. "Good thinking. Take Aldis with ye, since we need more than one. I wish ye to carry the beasties inside yer surcoat if ye can. Dinna be putting them in a bag or handling them roughly, understand?"

Valan shot him a disbelieving roll of his eyes. Ross could tell his brother thought him mad. He didn't care. This was the only thing he could think of that might bring Elise a smile. He turned to Elliott. "We shall go to the houses around the village and see if any of the crofters have cats to spare."

"Aye, m'lord." Elliott's face went red as if he held his breath.

"What, Elliott?" Ross hoped the lad had enough sense not to act like Valan. He would hate to knock him on his arse.

"Since we're separating, what if we all come back with cats?"

"Then we will have many cats and few mice or rats." Ross eyed the young man, daring him to argue.

Elliott gave an obedient bow. "Aye, m'lord. When do we leave?"

"Now."

The four of them headed to the stables without a word to anyone else. Munro took charge of the keep, ready with a tale should anyone ask questions. Something about Ross craving roasted bawties for supper. A hunt for the mountain hares seemed plausible enough. When they returned home with cats rather than rabbits, they would worry about their lies then. They charged across the glen as though heading into battle.

Valan and Aldis split off and headed for the miller as Ross and Elliott thundered toward the nearest waddle and daub hut that looked to keep livestock. Anyone attempting to protect their fodder and grain from rodents might have cats or kittens to spare. They slowed as they neared the home so as not to alarm the residents.

"Look!" Elliott pointed at a fine-looking tiger-striped feline sunning on top of a fence rail. "Now that there's a braw-looking moggy."

"With any luck, they'll be willing to part with it," Ross said. He'd brought enough silver to pay for a horse. Surely, he had enough to purchase a cat.

The man of the house blocked the doorway with his scythe held at the ready. He didn't speak, but then again, he didn't have to. His scowl spoke for him.

"I be Commander Ross MacDougall." Ross halted his horse far enough from the man to give him some ease. "*Gallóglaigh* to the Lord of Argyll."

The man made a respectful dip of his chin but held fast to his grain-cutting blade. "M'lord."

Nothing to do but get to the meat of it. Ross jerked a thumb toward the feline still sunning on the fence. "I am in need of a cat or two to rid my home of vermin. Do ye have one ye'd be willing to part with?"

"A cat?" the man repeated, squinting one eye shut as if sorely confused.

"Or two," Elliott said. "We have mice in the tower and the stable."

The crofter turned and spoke to someone inside the house, then stepped outside and closed the door. He leaned the scythe up against the wall and waved them forward. "Ye canna have old Tom there. Best mouser I've got and meaner than the devil himself." He pointed at the ramshackle building behind his home. "But a sleek little moggy had a litter in the loft. Four, I believe, but they're too young to leave her. Dinna even have their eyes open yet."

"Think we might catch her? I'll take her and the wee ones." Ross pulled the pouch of silver from his belt and rattled it. "I mean to pay ye well for yer troubles."

The man became a great deal friendlier. He wet his lips while eyeing the money. "The wife has a covered basket that'll do just fine to carry them. I'll fetch it, aye?"

Ross nodded but kept tight hold of the payment. "Once we have mother cat and her wee beasties safe and well in the basket, this bag of silver is yers."

With a nod, the crofter grinned. "All the animals love my daughter. Leannan will catch them for ye, I grant ye that."

After some stealthy maneuvering by the wee lass, Ross and Elliott soon found themselves headed home with a yowling mother cat and four mewling kittens. They rode as slow as possible, so as not to jostle the upset thing any more than necessary. The last thing he wanted was to present his lady love with a basket exploding with feline fury when they arrived.

Valan and Aldis arrived back at the keep at the same time. Each of them held a covered basket balanced in front of them.

"How many?" Ross hazarded to ask.

Both men grinned with pride. "Two mothers with fine healthy litters. One has six wee ones. The other five. The miller swears they breed the best mousers this side of Scotland."

Ross swallowed hard. Three mama cats. Fifteen kittens. God's beard. He rolled his shoulders. Elise wanted cats. She now had plenty.

"Do we have enough mice to keep them all alive?" Elliott asked in a hushed tone.

"I dinna ken." Ross made a mental note to place a guard on the new chicks just hatched out. "Tell Munro to fetch some saucers of cream and whatever extra fat and meat scraps he can spare. Else we'll not have a chick left to our names, and Elise will have me arse."

"We can try to keep them all in the tower," Elliott suggested. "With the nights still brisk, they should like being inside by the fire. That should give the hens a fighting chance to get their broods a little grown, ye ken?"

Ross pulled in a deep breath and blew it out. "Aye. Get Aldis to help ye see them comfortable on the third floor in one of the bedchambers. Make certain the hearth's well lit, then bring me word when all is well. I will show them to Lady Elise once they're all settled." He gave the lad a pointed look. "Alive, healthy, and happy, aye?"

The young man gave an understanding bob of his head, dismounted, and gently took the basket of yowling cats from Ross.

Ross dismounted, handed the reins to a stable lad, and watched Aldis and Elliott tote the three baskets inside.

"I never thought I'd live to see the day when ye did such a

thing," Valan said as he stepped up beside him.

"Neither did I." Ross hoped the plan would at least give Elise a happy distraction until God blessed her womb with a child. He realized cats and kittens could never replace a bairn, but he prayed they'd make her smile a little. "Maybe someday ye will understand, brother."

Valan shook his head. "I hope not." He jerked a thumb toward the skirting wall. "I believe I'll take the high ground for a while. Let me know if ye need anything else, ye ken?"

"Valan." Ross stopped him. "I thank ye."

His brother gave a lopsided smile, then continued onward.

After a deep fortifying breath, Ross went inside, glancing around for any sign of Elise. All seemed quiet and calm. Apparently, she still rested in her chambers.

Aldis and Elliott came trotting down the stairs, then gave him a nod. "The first bedchamber," Aldis called out.

"They're cozy as can be," Elliott added. "Munro's taking up their food now."

Ross thumped his chest in thanks, then headed upstairs. When he reached the solar door, he lightly tapped on it rather than enter without warning. With Elise's shyness during their first few weeks of marriage, he'd ordered a privacy screen built around the corner holding the chamber pot and washstand. But since it was Elise's monthly time, her needs required more consideration whether the screen sheltered her or not.

"Elise?"

"Come in, Ross."

When he eased open the door, his heart sank.

She sat in the armchair beside the window, staring out as if trapped in a lonely trance.

"I have a surprise for ye, m'love," he said softly. "Feel ye well enough to go upstairs with me?"

"Upstairs?" she repeated without looking away from the window. "Whatever for?"

"'Tis a surprise. Come with me, aye? Up to the first bedchamber." He held his breath, hoping she'd indulge him.

She turned and fixed him with a quizzical frown. "I thought the third floor was already done? What else could ye do?"

"Come and see."

With a weary huff, she pushed up from the chair and joined him at the door. "Did ye forget I wished to rest until supper?" she gently scolded.

"This canna wait." Allowing her to take the lead, he followed her up the winding staircase. When they reached the door, he held her back. "Close yer eyes."

First, she rolled them, then she complied.

He pushed open the door and steered her inside, pleased to see that Munro and the lads had done well. A cheery fire crackled in the hearth, and piles of hay and bundles of rags had been strategically placed around the room. The trio of baskets sat propped on their sides with their lids secured open. Three bowls of milk and two trenchers of meat scraps sat on the floor at the far wall. A black and gray striped cat, a nearly solid gray cat, and one that looked as if God had painted it with every leftover color in his kingdom crouched in front of the bowls, eating their fill and flipping their tails back and forth. "Open yer eyes, my love."

The corners of Elise's mouth trembled upward. "Ye found us three fine cats." Then she frowned. "But why are they up here?"

"They each have kittens." He hadn't a clue how old the other two litters were, but at this point, it didn't matter. "Too young to be in the stable yet. Dinna even have their eyes open. I thought we'd let them settle in here for a while until they know this place to be their home."

Her confused frown deepened. "How many kittens?"

He pointed to the gray and black striped cat. "That one has four, I know. Elliott and I found her. Then one of the others has six and one has five."

Elise's lips parted as she turned back and stared at the three mama cats. "That's fifteen kittens. Eighteen cats in all."

"Aye." 'Twas just his luck. She would be better at numbers

than most.

She pressed her fingers to her mouth. He couldn't decide if she meant to laugh or cry.

Then she laughed—or giggled quietly as she eased around the room. With an incredulous glance back in his direction, she shook her head. "Eighteen cats? All because…" Her voice trailed off as she scooped up a wee mewling ball of fur and cuddled it to her cheek.

"Because I love ye." He shrugged. "I didna ken what else to do to make ye smile. I love ye so much. Ye're all that matters to me, dear one."

She placed the fluffy mite back into the nest of rags with its siblings, then ran to him and held him tight. "I love ye, Ross." She peered up at him, her eyes glistening with unshed tears. "And as long as I have ye, I will always consider myself blessed."

He closed his eyes, held her close, and thanked God above for every single cat in that room.

CHAPTER EIGHT

"**M**ERCIFUL HEAVENS, THAT'S a powerful smell." Elise shielded her nose and mouth as she and Florie stood just inside *the cat room*, as dubbed by all in the keep. Even with the soiled hay removed each day and fresh provided, the place still reeked. Ross's decision to house eighteen cats in one bedchamber failed to consider that wee moggies did not use chamber pots. Eyes squinted against the acrid aroma, she propped the mop and broom against the wall and set the bucket of wash water beside them. "With the weather warmer and the wee ones scampering about like wild beasties, they'll be just fine in the stable. What say we move them? Today?"

"Let me throw open the window first." Florie held her nose and scurried across the room, dodging the furry obstacles as they tried to catch hold of her skirts. She secured the tapestry covering the window over to the side and threw open the shutters.

Elise filled her apron with kittens and nodded for Florie to do the same. "Their mamas will follow us. I hope. That'll give us fewer trips." The plan worked well enough, but it still took two rounds to get all the future mousers moved.

"But we'll still allow them back in the keep now and then?" Florie cuddled an orange kitten close. Its purring rumbled as loud as a cat four times its size.

"Of course." Elise knew Florie had a fondness for that one in particular, and he followed the maid around the keep like a devoted little dog.

The smiling lass tucked the little ginger cat back in the straw with its mother. The feisty thing shoved its littermates aside, latched on to a teat, and worked its tiny paws in a kneading motion as mama cat lazily licked her paws as if bored with the entire chore of feeding her offspring.

As they exited the stable, a flurry of excitement outside the newly installed portcullis slowed them to a halt. Ross shouted for the iron gate to be raised. Valan and a man Elise didn't recognize rode inside, dismounted, then rushed to Ross's side.

"That canna be good," Florie observed. She tugged on Elise's arm. "We best get inside, m'lady. If anything's gone awry, the commander will wish ye safe inside the tower."

Something about Ross's pained expression as he looked her way made her decide otherwise. "Nay. I will go to my husband's side until he shoos me away." She motioned Florie toward the door. "On wi' yerself, though. Tell Munro Valan's back. I'm sure the man will be starving. Ye know he's a bottomless pit."

"Aye, m'lady." The maid scurried up the steps, stumbling as she kept looking back at the trio of men gathered in the bailey.

Elise drew in a deep breath and marched forward, determined to remain calm. The men went silent as soon as she came within earshot. A dark omen, indeed. "Ye might as well tell me," she said, eyeing each of them as she joined them. "I can tell something's amiss."

Ross stared at her for entirely too long, the set of his mouth and the worry in his eyes chilling her to the bone. "Craevan is at Dunstaffnage Castle."

She blinked then swayed back a step, her head and her heart whirling at the terrible possibilities those words unleashed. Ross caught her and pulled her close.

"It cannot be," she whispered, unable to accept the reality of such a dark prospect. "How...how did he find me?" She had escaped the man when he headed south in search of that ridiculous treasure. Weeks and weeks she stole her way across

Ireland before O'Conor captured her and made her a slave in his household. How could Craevan have found her when he hadn't even known her to be gone?

"It appears when he returned to his estate and discovered ye missing, he not only searched all over Ireland but posted a reward and sent word of it far and wide," Valan said. "O'Conor got wind of it and told him all he knew." His jaw tightened as his focus shifted back to his brother. "Feckin' bastard probably counted it as a bonus to the cruel farce he had already played upon the two of ye the first time."

"And Craevan brought his solicitor," said the man she had never met. He gave a polite bow. "Liam Galleon, m'lady. Forgive us for bringing such dire news to yer door on this fine spring day."

She attempted to wet her lips and give a polite reply, but her mouth went dry as dust. Instead, she nodded and managed a weak smile. If Craevan waited at Dunstaffnage, then the Lord of Argyll knew her marriage contract to Ross meant nothing. Her stomach churned, threatening to expel the bannock and cheese she'd eaten to break her fast. The Lord of Argyll's opinion of her mattered little. What the Lady of Argyll thought about her meant everything. She tightened her hold on Ross. "I am not well at all," she whispered. "Might ye help me inside?"

Without a word, he scooped her up and cradled her to his chest. As he walked, he stared straight ahead, the line of his jaw hard as stone.

Every plan she considered to counter this terrible turn seemed doomed to fail. With her head tucked to his chest, she marked his pounding heartbeats to hold fast to what little calmness she still possessed. "What shall we do?" When he didn't answer, she fisted his tunic in her hand and thumped it against him. "What *can* we do?"

"We must face him and demanded an annulment." Ross shouldered open the door. Everyone in the main hall scattered. Bad news traveled fast. He took a step toward the stairwell, then paused. "If he willna agree to an annulment, I will challenge him."

"I wouldna have ye soil yer hands or yer soul with his blood."

He ignored her words and kept climbing the stairs. With a hard kick, he knocked open the door and eased her down on their couch. She pressed shaking hands to her brow and massaged, grinding her fingers into her temples to ease the pounding ache in her head.

"Ye are *my* wife, and I will never allow another man to take ye." He sat beside her and pulled her into his arms. Stroking her hair, he nuzzled his cheek against the top of her head and held her tighter. "Mine."

As she lay in his arms, wrestling with the torment, a plan unfolded in her mind as if gifted by angels. "He doesna want me," she said, careful to reason out every angle of what she wished to attempt. Near as she could tell, her plot appeared solid. "He wants the fake treasure my stepmother planted in his mind." She tapped a finger on Ross's chest, mulling out what they should do. "If I can make him believe I'll reveal the treasure once he signs the annulment, he should go away and bother us no more."

"Too simple. He'll nay be so likely to wander off on another fool's errand." Ross made an ominous popping of his knuckles. "I prefer a more *permanent* solution."

She knew what *permanent* meant. "We shouldna kill him. Thou shalt not kill—remember?"

"I feel certain God would understand in this case." Even though Ross had carried her with an endearing gentleness, she felt the tautness of his strength as he held her. The hardness of his tensed muscles. The man longed to attack. "Besides," he said. "Are we not already committing adultery?"

Fair point, but she ignored it. "Help me come up with a tale about the treasure. A story he'll swallow, so he'll agree to the annulment." Sadly, she had never been all that good at telling believable lies.

"What is it he already believes?"

"I canna say for sure. My stepmother didna feel the need to share the deception with me." She tried to remember everything Craevan ever shouted at her while frustrated about finding the elusive treasure. "I remember him saying my mother hid it while a young girl in Ireland."

Ross pursed his lips and stared out into space. "But ye dinna ken where or what *it* might be?"

"I have no idea." She released a frustrated sigh and pushed herself upright on the couch. "Jewels? Coin? What else could it be?"

He didn't answer. Just sat there with a thoughtful scowl. His eyes narrowed to slits.

"Ross?"

"Yer mother hid it whilst a young girl in Ireland," he repeated. "Close to where she grew up, I suppose?"

She gave another impatient snort. "He never told me exactly what Arnella said, and she never said anything to me because of..." She brushed the mark on her cheek, the curse she rarely noticed anymore because Ross made her feel beautiful, and everyone else in the keep never paid it any mind. "She feared me, but I didna have the sense at the time to use it to my advantage."

"Then perhaps we should come up with a more believable tale." Ross jumped up as if too excited to sit. "We could use the excuse that ye wouldna tell him before because he treated ye so cruelly and made ye hate him. But now ye're willing to share it because ye've found love and wish him to leave ye be in yer new life."

With Craevan's frustration and greed used to their advantage, surely, they could sell him the new lie with little trouble. "My mother was from just north of Kildare. We could say she hid it somewhere in that area."

Ross stopped pacing, faced her, and smiled. "Or we could say ye recovered it when ye ran and still have it in yer possession."

"But the earl caught me and made me a slave." She bowed her head and closed her eyes at the humiliating memory. "He had me stripped and beaten to ensure I understood my place." She rubbed her arms to erase the filth her captors left behind. "And he said he wanted the demon that marked me to know its place as well. Then they gave me back my clothes and tossed me in with the others."

Rage flashed across Ross's face. "If ye had a keepsake with ye, could ye have hidden it when ye realized ye were about to be taken?"

She shook her head. "The earl's brutes came upon me in a wood whilst chasing down a rival clan. I didna see them until it was too late."

"But would Craevan believe ye hid something in that wood out of fear someone from his household might pursue ye?" Ross cocked a brow, a sly knowing in his grin easing the knot in her chest.

"He might." She chewed on her bottom lip, remembering the vile fool's desperation to fill his empty coffers. "He was skint broke last summer. I wouldna think he'd be any better now." Rising from the couch, she moved to the window and pulled in a deep breath of fresh spring air. "In fact,..." She drew on the peacefulness of the glen coming to life with its lush carpet of green and early blooms coaxed forth by the sun's warmer touch. "I can only wonder how he afforded a solicitor to accompany him to Dunstaffnage. I'm sure he's desperate by now."

Ross came up behind her, encircled her with both arms, and hugged her back against his chest. "Who's to say the man is a real solicitor? Just because Craevan claims it doesna mean it's so."

She hadn't considered that and scolded herself for taking Craevan at his word. Just because she found it difficult to lie didn't mean that cur felt the same. "What shall our treasure be?"

"A wee Irish lass wouldna hide gold or silver coin." Ross rubbed his cheek against her hair, mussing her braid, but she didn't care. "A family heirloom for certain. Necklace or a pin, perhaps?"

"Maybe a gemstone set in gold or silver?" But what would be

dear enough to make Craevan crazed for it? Elise knew nothing of jewelry, and truth be told, had never desired it. She valued a roof and food for those she cared about more than any trinkets. "What would he value most?"

Ross chuckled. The warm rumbling of his mirth tickled up her back. "Anything that would hook him. How about a fine gold brooch encrusted with emeralds, rubies, sapphires, and pearls?"

She smiled, relaxing back against him. "Mama would laugh if she heard such. She came from a poor family."

"Maybe so, but if he believed she hid treasure once, it shouldna be that difficult to convince him again." Ross kissed her cheek. "We must go to Dunstaffnage tomorrow, ye ken?"

Even with the sun warming her, she shivered, suddenly chilled to the bone. "What if the Lord of Argyll seizes me and hands me over afore we can make Craevan accept our lie?" She feared the man wouldn't fall for another tall tale so easily. Greedy, he might be, and stupid, but he could very well demand to set eyes on the treasure before granting the annulment. Then what would they do? "Ye know Lord Toad has never liked me."

"I will not allow that to happen." He cradled her close as if content to stand there forever. "And I wager Lady Christiana wouldna allow it either."

"I fear she will think less of me for not telling anyone about Craevan. Especially not her." Although she'd never had an opportunity to speak with the woman before marrying Ross. She had sent many notes of thanks to the lady since but never had she talked with her face to face. "Ye said yerself we should never anger her."

"She'll ken well enough that ye held yer tongue because ye knew no one would listen."

True enough, but she still prayed the fine lady remained her ally. And if she didn't, if all at Dunstaffnage sided with Craevan, she would do whatever necessary to keep her and Ross's happiness safe.

⟫⟫⟫⟪⟪⟪

ROSS CLENCHED HIS jaw and turned away as Elise hugged Florie like she would never see her again. Both women made sad, chirping sounds that ripped at his heart.

"Elise—we must go." He gave her arm a gentle tug, unable to bear anymore. The two were like mourners making their last farewells.

"I'll make certain Munro doesna cut the herbs too close," Florie promised, her bottom lip trembling as she backed away.

"See that ye do." Elise's voice quivered, but she managed a smile and a fluttering wave.

When she turned and reached for him to help her into the saddle, Ross thanked God above. Drawing out this departure only made the ominous cloud of what lay ahead darker and more difficult to face.

"I am sorry," she whispered as he lifted her into the saddle. "I guess my courage waits until later to make a grand showing."

He gave her an encouraging smile. "We willna fail, m'love. No one takes what is mine. Not ever." He pressed a kiss to her hand, then patted her knee. "Shall we be about it then?"

She lifted her chin and squared her shoulders. "I am ready, husband."

Ross settled atop his mount and led the way out the gate. Elise knew their plan, but little did she know he had a second idea if their first ploy failed. They would be free of Craevan one way or another.

As soon as they cleared the narrow barbican connecting the new gatehouse, he paused for her to draw alongside and ride on his left, so he might protect her if need be. With the mild day and wind at their backs, they would arrive at Dunstaffnage by late afternoon. Vallan and Liam had already returned to the Lord of Argyll's court. Those two, as well as Thorburn and Adellis, would provide at least four trusted allies should they need them. But they wouldn't.

Ross rested his hand on the purse tied to his belt. It contained enough gold to tempt any man. If Craevan had any sense about him, he'd listen to reason, take the gold, and sign off on the annulment. If it came to pass that he had no sense, Ross had a dagger to show the man the error of his ways.

Neither spoke, but the silence as they rode took on the feel of a strong, united front. The closer they drew to Dunstaffnage, the more often he sidled glances at Elise.

"Ye can stop watching to see if I faint dead away or fall off my horse," she observed while staring straight ahead. "I willna give Craevan the satisfaction of doing such a thing."

"Tell me about the man so I'll know what to expect." The bastard's particulars mattered little, but he sensed if he kept her talking, she would be all the better for it.

"I canna think of words vile enough to describe him." Her violent shudder lent credence to her opinion. "Greedy. Selfish. Cutthroat. Repulsive." With another twitch of her shoulder, she made a face as if she smelled a horrible stench. "Anything low and despicable. He is a vile man. Even his name suggests sinful rot."

"Good."

"Good?" She stared at him as if he'd gone simple in the head. "And how is any of that good?"

"Lady Christiana despises everything ye just described." With a self-assured wink, he increased their pace. "'Twill strengthen our case."

"I pray ye are right." Her worried gaze shifted to the castle looming ahead.

Waves crashing against the shore welcomed them back to Dunstaffnage. The breeze carried the familiar tang of the sea. A line of darker clouds blotted out the sky over the frothy waves. Ross prayed the gathering storm wasn't an ill omen. As they entered the outer bailey, the wind picked up, shoving at their backs as if hurrying them toward their fate.

Valan met them at the entrance to the inner courtyard. Eyes

sparkling with a wicked glint, his smugness strengthened Ross's resolve. "'Tis only the man and his solicitor," he said. "The guards he brought deserted him. Headed back to Ireland this morning."

"Why?" Ross asked, helping his wife dismount.

"Ye ken as well as I that soldiers need paying." Valan snorted as he motioned for them to follow. "They tired of hearing *someday* and *soon as I find that treasure.*"

"Good. That should rattle him enough to open his ears to reason."

"He has never been a reasonable man," Elise said. "If anything, it will make his desperation more reckless."

"That still benefits us, m'love." Ross caught hold of his brother's arm and halted him. "What of the MacDougall? I assume since he welcomed the man into his hall, he sides with him?"

"I'm nay so sure." Valan's eyes narrowed to a thoughtful slant. "While 'tis true our liege allowed the man entry, he has said nothing to encourage him." His thoughtfulness turned mischievous. "Of course, the Lady Christiana has stuck to his side both yesterday and today." He grinned at Elise. "It appears Her Ladyship protects ye still, dear sister."

"I canna understand why." Elise leaned to peer around Valan, fixing a pained look on the arched double doors. "I've never spoken to the woman directly. Why would she give a whit if I draw breath or not?"

"I wondered the same," Valan said. "Until her sister arrived late yesterday."

"She has a sister?" Ross tried to recall the woman but couldn't.

"Aye." Valan's gaze dropped. After an uncomfortable glance at Elise, he paused and nudged a rock with the toe of his boot. Finally, his words came out strained as if confessing a terrible sin. "Lady Rhea, sister to Lady Christiana, bears a mark on her face verra similar to yers, m'lady." He winced and avoided eye contact. "Forgive me, my fine sister. I merely wished to offer an explanation as to why Lady Christiana aligns with ye as she does."

"I take no offense, Valan." Elise rested her hand on his arm. "But I thank ye for explaining Lady Christiana's generous protection."

"Let us hope that protection holds fast." Ross nodded toward the doors, the same fierce urgency pounding through him as when he faced battle. Truth be told, he did. A battle for the one he loved. A battle he refused to lose.

Elise's grip on his arm tightened, betraying her fears. He wished he could somehow console her, but the only way to wipe away her worries was to challenge them.

As they entered the hall, the focus of all in the room shifted to them. More men and women than usual for this time of day loitered in the large meeting area. The gossiping vultures added fuel to Ross's simmering rage. The grovelers probably laid in wait ever since Craevan's arrival.

The seats upon the dais were empty. The Lord and Lady of Argyll stood near a table, sorting through several parchments. A veiled woman lingered beside Lady Christiana, leaning close to share a private word. Ross assumed the woman to be Lady Rhea. The gossamer weave of the material covering the lady's face failed at hiding the deep red mark completely. The mottled patch started just below her left eye, then spread downward. The veil softened the feature, making it look more like a shadow, but to those who knew what to look for—the mark was still there.

Elise's fingers dug into his arm to the point of being painful. As gently as he could, he loosened her grip, then patted her hand.

With a polite nod, he greeted his liege. "M'lord."

"Commander." The MacDougall cast a knowing look at his wife, then cleared his throat. "Yer brother informed ye of the news we received?"

"Aye." Ross resettled his stance, then jutted his chin higher. "Where is this bastard who claims to have rights to my wife?"

The MacDougall's mustache barely twitched, but Lady Christiana's smile blossomed like a rose in full bloom. Even Lady Rhea's eyes sparkled and crinkled at the corners with approval unhidden by her veil.

"Fetch the Earl of Craevan and his solicitor," the MacDougall ordered. "If they're sober enough to walk."

Ross appreciated that information. "Yer guests unable to handle yer fine MacDougall whisky?"

"They are nay my guests," the lord retorted. "And they canna handle anything." He motioned them closer and pointed at the parchments on the table. "Our solicitor has reviewed the man's documents and found them wanting."

"Then why do we waste our time here?"

Elise squeezed his arm and drew closer as if to shush him.

He gave her the slightest shake of his head. "Nay, m'love. We have every right to ask such. There's much to be done at Tórrelise now that spring has arrived." Standing taller, he fixed a hard gaze on the MacDougall and added, "Our lives are to be lived. Savored. Not frittered away on things that dinna matter."

She hitched in a sharp breath.

The MacDougall's ruddy brows knotted in a frown. "We are here because I would think a wise man would wish all questions about his marriage settled." He tapped on the bottom of one of the pages. "Is this yer mark, Lady Elise?"

Ross willed her to say, "no." He even covered her hand with his, hoping she would understand his silent signal.

Her bewildered shrug strengthened his hope. "I canna say for certain, m'lord." She leaned closer and examined the document, then straightened. "When he forced me to make a mark on the marriage contract, my hands were tied behind my back." She nodded toward the other parchment. "I wasna allowed to sign my name as I did when I married Ross."

For the first time since joining the others at the table, Ross examined the document. The Earl of Craevan's contract had a disjointed *x* where Elise's signature belonged. "Anyone couldha made that mark."

"I agree," the Lord of Argyll said. "I ordered him to produce the holy man who performed the rite, or proof of where it had been recorded either in the church or in Edinburgh." He gave the document a disgruntled flick of his finger. "The man did neither." One side of his mustache twitched higher in a wily grin. "At least, while sober."

"Then again, the question begs to be asked, why the hell do we waste our time with this fool?" Ross smelled a trap, but he couldn't quite place it. "If yer solicitor deems Craevan's contract void, that settles the matter, aye?"

"Ye disappoint me, Commander Ross," Lady Christiana said. "I wouldha thought a proud warrior such as yerself would wish to defend his lady love and avenge all slurs lodged upon her."

A pair of MacDougall guards entered the hall, dragging a belligerent man between them. "Release me, I say! The devil's maid can wait until I am ready to receive her."

Bloodlust surged through Ross. "Devil's maid?" he repeated slowly. With a gentleness his rage barely allowed, he set Elise aside and strode closer. "Choose yer next words with care. Yer feckin' life depends on it."

The guards shoved the drunkard forward. The man lurched to the table, smacked both hands atop it, and jutted his head back and forth as if about to vomit. Slight of build and as bald as a boulder, he squinted at all in the room, then bared his yellowed, oversized teeth at Ross. "Who the hell do ye claim to be?"

"I dinna *claim* to be anyone," Ross retorted. "I *am* Ross Mac-Dougall, commander to the Lord of Argyll's tenth unit of *Gallóglaigh* warriors." He leaned closer so the bleary-eyed fool could focus on him. "And I am husband to Lady Elise."

"She is my property," the man sputtered. "Used the last of my money to buy that bitch, and she's yet to earn it out for me. Devil's mark or no, I got my due coming!"

"Ye've got it coming, all right." Ross's guttural roar shook the rafters as he upended the table in a hard upward thrust and slammed it into the man's face. No one insulted his Elise. No one.

"Ross!"

Elise started toward him, but he held up a hand to stop her.

"Nay, m'love." He rounded the mess and yanked the man up by the throat.

Blood spurted from the scoundrel's nose. He twisted and clawed to be free, blubbering obscenities unfit to be uttered in front of the ladies. Ross tightened his hold, squeezing off the man's air until he worried more about breathing than cursing. "Ye willna treat our ladies with such disrespect."

Valan stepped to Elise's side and eased her well out of harm's way. "Come, good sister. Let yer champion deal with this filth, ye ken?"

Ross gave his brother a nod of thanks. Valan understood and would keep Elise safe while he dealt with this cur. He threw the man to the floor.

"She is my wife," Craevan wheezed, crouching like the mongrel he was. "My wife. My property. Bought and paid for."

"I have evidence that shows otherwise," Lady Christiana said, her voice ringing loud with righteousness. She snapped her fingers, and a maid rushed forward with a small trunk clutched to her chest. Her ladyship made a polite tip of her head toward Ross, then smiled at Elise. "It serves for a married woman to keep the proof of her union's consummation. Since Lady Elise's new home required much work, her proof remained safe here at Dunstaffnage." She lifted the trunk's lid and pulled out a folded piece of linen. With a hard shake, she and the maid stretched it out between them, revealing the small bloodstain at its center. "Proof that the Lady Elise came as a virgin to Commander Ross." She turned and glared at the earl, still crouched beside the upended table. "Yer union was never consummated, and the marriage contract doesna bear the lady's full signature. Ye have no case in Argyll, all of Scotland, or any land 'neath the watchful eye of our Almighty God."

The Lord of Argyll stepped forward. "Admit it, Craevan." He held up the marriage contract. "Not only did ye leave the Lady Elise a virgin, but ye didna even bother to have yer supposed union recorded. Ye admitted so yerself whilst so deep in yer cups, ye couldna find yer arse with both hands."

Craevan squinted up at them all, then swiped the back of his hand across his bloody face. He fumbled with the top of his boot, yanked out a dagger, and lobbed it at Elise.

Ross stepped into the spinning dagger's path. The drunkard's faulty throw bounced the blade off his chest. He caught the knife before it hit the floor, flipped it, and shot it back at the man. "'Tis yer blade. Keep it."

Satisfaction filled Ross as the steel embedded itself to the hilt in Craevan's throat.

Eyes wide, mouth moving without any sound, the man sprawled sideways and went still.

"Well done, Commander," the MacDougall said as if Ross had just won a contest. "I had hoped for such an ending when I sent yer brother to fetch ye." He gave a polite tip of his head to his wife and sister-in-law. "Ye might say my eyes were opened to the error of my ways before." He looked back at Elise and then to Ross. "Ye know I never apologize. But as a proper penance for my misdeeds, speak with me later. After the feast. Ye shall not go unrewarded for yer loyalty and patience."

"Loyalty and patience?" Ross eyed the man. Had the MacDougall gone soft in the head? "I defended the woman I love, m'lord." As far as he cared, he and Elise would ride back to Tórrelise within the hour.

"Aye, maybe so." The MacDougall said with a grin at his wife. "But ye won a bet for me, man. And I rarely win a bet with Lady Christiana."

"Dinna gloat, Alexander," Lady Christiana said with a delicate sniff. "'Tis unbecoming of a man of yer status."

"Thank ye, m'lady," Elise said, stepping forward and offering a grateful curtsy. "For everything."

"Ye are most welcome, Lady Elise." The Lady of Argyll waved her forward. "Come. Join my sister and me. Let us leave the men to clear up this mess, aye?"

When she hesitated and glanced his way, Ross agreed with a

smile. They could talk later. In bed. And who knows? Perhaps God would also bless the day with the successful seeding of a bairn. "Dinna be sharing any of yer tricks with her, Lady Christiana," he called after them.

Lady Christiana answered with a graceful flutter of her hand.

"Ye're doomed," the McDougall remarked as he motioned for the guards to drag Craevan's body away. He softened the edict with a shrug and a wink. "Welcome to a life of servitude, m'lad. It's nay so bad once ye get used to it."

CHAPTER NINE

E LISE LIFTED HER face to the steady breeze blowing in from the sea. She supposed she should close the window against the cool night air, but the flickering of the stars as the waves crashed against the shore soothed her. "Was it wrong that we stayed the night and feasted rather than return home?" she asked without turning away from the peaceful view. "I almost feel guilty about celebrating my freedom." A winking point of light close to the moon caught her attention as if urging complete honesty. "Ye know I planned to kill him myself, but now I'm nay so sure I couldha done it."

"And that is why I am here, m'love." Ross slid her chemise off her shoulder and pressed a lingering kiss to her bare skin.

His warm lips held the power to make her forget everything but him.

"And I'm here to protect ye," he added, nibbling higher, up her neck, then behind her ear. "But most of all, I'm here to love ye."

She closed her eyes and leaned back, giving herself to his touch. A lazy giggle escaped her.

"Ye find me amusing?"

She turned in his arms, slid her hands up the smooth, hard ridges of bare chest, and hugged herself tight against the length of him. "Nay, m'love. I laughed because I had feared if I left the window open, we might grow too cold." Stretched high on her tiptoes, she teased the tip of her tongue along his collarbone while reaching down to wrap her fingers around his rigid shaft. A smile interrupted her licking when he shivered. "I dinna think catching a chill will be a problem for us this night. Do ye?"

"Not at all, my own." He gathered up her shift, slipped it off over her head, and tossed it away.

As he smoothed his hands down her back, then took tighter hold of her behind, she looped a leg around him and teased her toes along his thigh. She battled with an aching greediness for him to take her. On the couch. On the floor. In the chair. Anywhere, as long he buried himself inside her. But she also wanted to savor him slowly. Touch him. Taste him. Indulge and enjoy every sensation as he did the same for her. To make herself wait, she eased downward, sliding down his leg as she knelt.

He groaned when she took him in her mouth. It still amazed her how something so hard could still be so velvety. She cupped his bollocks in one hand and pumped with the other as she suckled him. With his fingers tangled in her hair, he held tight, groaning and gasping as she served him. His sounds excited her, making every part of her ache for relief.

"I can take no more," he growled as he stepped back, then joined her on the floor. Crouching on all fours, he licked a circle around her nipple, then drew it deep into his mouth with an urgent pulling. Fiery sparks shot through her. She hugged him tighter to her breasts. With one arm wrapped around her, he leaned her back. Still at her breast, he slid his fingers inside her.

"So wet," he whispered, his beard tickling as he shifted to the other breast while working his fingers deeper.

"Make me wetter," she begged in a breathless whisper, giving into the greed of wanting him inside her. "Take me."

He rolled her to her back and buried himself. Without drawing back out, he worked his hips and nuzzled along the line of her jaw. "I thought to go slowly, but I canna wait, m'love," he rasped across her lips. "Never will I ever get enough of ye."

"Never will ye have to," she promised, raking her fingers

down his back as she wrapped her legs around him. "I tried to be patient and savor ye, but this..." She worked her own hips and squeezed. "This is what I wanted." She nipped his bottom lip. "Ye couldha bent me over the windowsill and took me right at the verra first, and it wouldha suited me as well."

Even in the shadows, she saw his grin.

"We shall do that next," he promised with a slow, teasing withdrawal, then thrust in again with a satisfying shove.

"A solid plan if ever I heard one." She matched his rhythm, then squeezed his buttocks with both hands, her silent signal to move faster.

"Aye, m'love. Gladly."

As he drove her over the edge of bliss, she silently thanked this beloved man for teaching her how to thrive.

EPILOGUE

Tórrelise Keep
Western Scotland
Early summer 1277

"IT WILLNA BE the same without ye fighting at my side." Valan eyed him, his blonde brows knotting in an unusual show of concern. A show of concern that irritated Ross to no end.

"I am not an invalid." He shifted on the bench and squinted against the glare almost blinding him. The brightness of the sunny day irritated him as well, but Elise insisted sunshine and fresh air would help strengthen him after that feckin' fever or ague or whatever it was had nearly sent him to the grave.

"At least ye will have more time with the bairn this way." Valan's tone still held too much indulgence for Ross's liking. "I ken he's only a wee thing of but a month, but he needs to get to know his da afore ye go traipsing off to battle. Remember how Mother always fussed about Da never being around 'til we were half-grown?"

"That she did." The memory made Ross smile, and as Elise emerged from the chicken coop with their son swaddled to her chest inside a length of plaid, a sense of peace and thankfulness filled him. So afraid of never having a child, she guarded their wee lad with fury, refusing to leave him in anyone's care but her own.

He resettled himself on the bench again, suddenly ashamed of pitying himself when he had so many blessings. "When do ye leave?"

"Day after next." Valan plucked a long strand of grass from the pot of flowers beside them. As he smoothed the blade between his fingers, he frowned down at it. "I hope to get the troops there within four days, but 'tis probably a fool's wish. With a score of men and extra supplies, I'm thinking 'twill be closer to a sennight afore we arrive." He tossed the grass aside and scowled at the smithy's forge. The rhythmic ring of hammer against steel filled the courtyard. "With Thorburn gone to Ireland and ye still in need of healing, finding myself in charge of all the *Gallóglaigh* concerns me."

"Ye've been in command before. Ye can do it again." Ross leaned back against the stone wall, the bothersome weariness nagging him again. "Did the MacDougall know how long the Maxwells held off the English afore sending for aid?"

Valan gave a wincing shrug. "He thinks at least a month. All he knows for certain is Laird Maxwell never returned from Wales, leaving his lady wife and daughter to hold the newly built keep."

"If it were me, I'd take the most seasoned men only." Ross made an effort to perk up as Elise headed their way. "Ye dinna wish to be dealing with those who might be more interested in the ladies than the battle."

"As if ye never chased the ladies?"

Ross shot his brother a silencing look as Elise joined them. Her coppery curls shone in the sunshine, strands fluttering around her flushed face. He swallowed hard, realizing that once he'd sworn to never take a wife. But now he couldn't imagine life without her. "And what does our son think of yer fine fat hens, m'love?" He stretched to peer inside the wrap. The peaceful sight of the sleeping babe melted his heart.

"As ye can see, he was quite impressed." Her smile faded into a worried frown. "Ye've grown weary. Come inside where ye can rest on the couch."

"I will not." With an unyielding tip of his head, he stared her down. "If I dinna push myself to regain my strength, I shall remain weak. Ye must let me take control of this in my own way." He kissed her hand and forced a softer tone. "Ye nursed me well over the winter. Even when ye shouldha been abed after birthing wee Gareth. But now 'tis my work that must be done, ye ken?"

"As long as ye understand 'tis my work to nag ye when ye do it wrong." She arched a brow, daring him to argue.

"I'm glad I'm off to defend Caerlaverock," Valan observed with a smug grin. "Me thinks 'tis a damn sight easier fighting the enemy than it is to be married."

"Yer time's comin'," Elise assured. She nudged Ross and nodded in Valan's direction. "Do ye not agree?"

Ross slid his arm around her waist and pulled her down into his lap. "Aye, m'love. I agree." He shot a knowing wink at Valan. "And it'll happen when ye least expect it."

About the Author

If you enjoyed A SCOT TO HAVE AND TO HOLD, please consider leaving a review on the site where you purchased your copy, or a reader site such as Goodreads, or BookBub.

If you'd like to receive my newsletter, here's the link to sign up: maevegreyson.com/contact.html#newsletter

I love to hear from readers! Drop me a line at: maevegreyson@gmail.com

Or visit me on Facebook: facebook.com/AuthorMaeveGreyson

Join my Facebook Group – Maeve's Corner: facebook.com/groups/MaevesCorner

I'm also on Instagram: maevegreyson

My website: https://maevegreyson.com

Feel free to ask questions or leave some Reader Buzz on: bingebooks.com/author/maeve-greyson

Follow me on these sites to get notifications about new releases, sales, and special deals:

Amazon: amazon.com/Maeve-Greyson/e/B004PE9T9U

BookBub: bookbub.com/authors/maeve-greyson

Many thanks, and may your life always be filled with good books!
Maeve